A MCKENZIE WEDDING

MCKENZIE BROTHERS #2

LEXI BUCHANAN

HFCA Publishing House

Ireland

www.lexibuchanan.net

First Published 2013

This Edition 2024

Cover Design: Alison Chaffin Higson

Editor: Sirena Van Schaik

BETA Readers: Emma Clifton, Heidy Bendana, Kristy Louise Garbutt,
Nadine Winningham

SYNOPSIS

You are cordially invited
to witness the marriage between
Michael McKenzie
and
Lily Redmond
1st August
McKenzie Ranch
Lexington, Kentucky

1

MICHAEL

SECONDS AWAY FROM CLIMAXING, I GRIPPED LILY'S HIPS AS she rocked back and forth. Despite the knots of pleasure tightening my muscles, I couldn't stop my legs from buckling slightly. I had no idea how my Harley was still holding us upright.

Lily moaned with pleasure as my cock bounced within her as she sat astride me, my cock buried deep within her. Her erect nipples rubbed against my chest as she rode me hard. I squeezed her rump with my hands, helping her move on me and taking me even deeper with each shift of her hips.

"Hold my hips," Lily demanded before leaning back over the handlebars.

Her sex tightened with her changed position, but it gave me free access to her beautiful body.

"Play with your nipples," I commanded, my eyes smoldering with desire as I dug my fingers into her hips, pinning her to my cock.

Lily slid her hands up slowly, her lips caught between her teeth, her eyes burning brightly under her thick lashes. A gasp escaped her kiss-bruised mouth as she began to massage and pinch her rosy nipples as I'd instructed.

The tightening of her sex mirrored each flick of her fingers, and I felt my orgasm building. Leaning forward, I buried my head in her chest and thrust into her with abandon. Lily's nails bit into my back, scoring my skin as my cock thrust in and out, building my orgasm to heights I never imagined. I stiffened and groaned, "Come for me, Lily," and was rewarded with spasms that sucked at my cock. My spine tingled, and my balls pulled up.

"Dammit!" I jerked awake as my cock twitched and shot semen onto my stomach. I grabbed my dick to finish my orgasm and slowly brought my breathing under control.

Fuck. I silently cursed to myself as I looked around the empty bedroom. That didn't count. There was no way I was going to admit anything to Lily. I'd promised her I wouldn't masturbate, but I couldn't control that dream. If I did have control, it was because I was so damn frustrated with Lily's "no sex for the week before the wedding" rule. Fuck. What Lily doesn't know won't hurt her, right?

Still feeling groggy from my early wake-up call, I snuck out of bed and went to the bathroom. I didn't look in the mirror when I stepped into the shower. Today was the day, and I could feel my nerves tingling with anticipation. Lily was finally going to be my wife. It hadn't arrived soon enough. I grinned as I caressed my still-alert penis, thinking about Lily. Even without the excruciating past week, I had been looking forward to our wedding for a month. I couldn't wait to slide my wedding ring onto her finger.

While Lily, my mom, and even Lucien had been planning the wedding, I tried to play an active role in the arrangements. For some reason, though, most of my suggestions sounded stupid. I would have been okay with a quick trip to Vegas, but I kept that idea to myself. I might have been able to convince Lily to elope, but I knew my mother would have ripped me to shreds for suggesting it.

After stepping out of the shower, I dried off and wrapped a towel around my waist. I walked back into the bedroom, only to come face-to-face with Lucien.

"What are you doing in here?"

"Making sure you don't get cold feet," Lucien replied, grinning as he reclined in the oversized blue chair by the window.

"Ha! You wish."

Lucien's silent gaze bore into my back, but I tried to shrug it off. It wasn't like my brother to be so quiet. When I turned toward him, I winced at the serious look on Lucien's face. "What?" I asked.

"I don't wish, Michael." Lucien ran his hands through his hair. I stayed silent, knowing my brother had more to say. "I love Lily. Like a sister. You know that."

I grinned. "Lucien, lighten up. I know that, okay? I admit that I found your relationship with Lily odd in the beginning, but I was only messing with you." I sighed and turned back to the closet. "Now that's settled, get out of here so I can get dressed in peace."

Without moving from his spot by the window, Lucien glanced out the curtains, then back at me.

He sighed again. "I'm staying in here to keep you

grounded. Besides, if I step foot out there, Mom is going to introduce me to all the single women. It gets tiring. I wish she'd leave me alone. I can find a woman on my own if I want one," he finished under his breath.

I chuckled as I pulled on my shorts and jeans, thinking about what my brother had said. Lucien didn't seem interested in finding a woman, and he hadn't been for a long time.

"Knock, knock," Ruben said cheerfully as he walked into the bedroom, looking just as relieved to have the door shut behind him as Lucien had been.

"What the fuck is wrong with everyone today? It's like Grand Central," I grumbled while pulling on a T-shirt.

The wedding wasn't for a few hours, so I'd planned on escaping for a while on one of the horses. Now, it didn't look like that was going to happen.

"Mom has it in her head that her four remaining sons need wives. Do you want me to go on?" Ruben grumbled, throwing himself on the bed.

I smirked. "No, I think I get the picture."

Try as I might, I couldn't wipe the grin from my face. Little did they know, Lily was looking for more female company for them. One reason was that she didn't like being outnumbered when we visited the ranch. The other reason was that she wanted my brothers to be as happy as we were. I was going to keep both facts to myself.

"I thought you had a date for the wedding?" I asked, shoving my feet into loafers.

Shaking his head, Ruben replied, "Bad idea. If you bring a woman to a wedding with your family, they start to get the wrong idea. We're all single except for Ramon, which is why Mom keeps trying to get us to help seat the guests. Mainly the single females."

I took the seat across from Lucien on the sofa, wondering why my brother had been quiet.

"Mom doesn't know when to quit," Lucien stated.

He seemed to be about to say something else when the bedroom door opened again. We stiffened, then collapsed in relief—it was only Ramon.

"Mom's five minutes behind me," he said, leaning against the door.

I snickered and moved Ramon away from the door just as someone knocked on it.

Looking at my brothers made me laugh because they looked ready to jump out the window. They all knew that knock—Mom.

"You're all being ridiculous, and you have Carla. So what is your problem?" I muttered to Ramon.

She knocked again.

I sighed and pulled the door open to meet my mom's angry expression.

"Are you hiding three of your brothers in here?" she asked, pushing her way in. She found Lucien, Ruben, and Ramon sneaking into the bathroom, which was comical, really.

"Well, really. How old are you boys, hiding from your poor old mama? Stop being ridiculous, and go out there and help your father."

"Yes, ma'am," said Ruben, hiding his laughter as he kissed Mom on the cheek and left the room. Lucien and Ramon followed in the same manner.

"Your breakfast will be ready in five minutes," she said as she slipped out the door.

Once the door was closed and I was finally alone again, I thought about Lily and hoped she was doing okay.

Occasionally, she would feel nauseous in the morning, so I'd get out of bed first, run down to the kitchen, and pour her a small glass of Canada Dry ginger ale. I'd also bring her some crackers, which she would nibble on until she started to feel better. So far, they seemed to be working.

Tradition said that I wasn't supposed to see Lily on our wedding day until she was walking toward me in her wedding dress, but nothing was said about texting each other. I needed to know that Lily was all right.

2

LILY

I slowly opened my eyes as I rolled onto my back. I really wanted to jump up and race down the hall to Michael's room and throw myself into his arms. I'd beg him to show me everything I'd been missing during this excruciatingly long week. Why had I come up with the no-sex-for-a-week rule?

I ground my teeth, buried my nose under the thick duvet, and counted the seconds as my stomach rolled and threatened to come racing up my throat. As much as I wanted to see Michael, I needed to wait for the nausea to settle. It usually did so within a few minutes, but Michael insisted on taking care of me.

He pampered me, saying it was his job to make sure I was well taken care of. Every time I tried to tell him that I could look after myself and didn't want him running around after me, he pointed out that I was carrying his child and that it was the least he could do.

I eventually realized that Michael really wanted to do everything to make sure I was comfortable, not because he felt obligated, but because he enjoyed being needed.

I smoothed my hands over my belly, which protected our children. Michael had no idea that I was carrying twins. The doctor told me after the sonogram when Michael was out of the room. Apparently, one of the babies had been lying alongside his or her brother or sister, making it more difficult to see.

Every time I thought about having twins, my heart skipped a beat. Having a small part of ourselves to look after within six months or so was daunting enough, but the idea of having two babies frightened the life out of me. Michael would probably panic at first, but I knew he would support me every step of the way, along with his family.

All I had to do was tell him about the twins but considering how stressed he'd been leading up to the wedding, I thought it best to wait until after we'd said, "I do."

Shaking myself from my thoughts, I realized the nausea had finally disappeared. Moving slowly to keep it at bay, I slid out from under the covers and made my way to the bathroom.

I turned on the shower, relieved myself, washed my hands, and brushed my teeth before climbing under the warm spray, which had reached the correct temperature.

Michael had been adamant that I do not shower in steaming water because he didn't think it was good for the baby to be "roasted."

I reached out and took hold of the shower gel, smiling as I squirted some into my palm. I placed the bottle back on the ledge.

I began rubbing the gel into my neck and collar-bone. I moved my hands over my engorged breasts and sensitive nipples. The pressure went straight to my clitoris, causing me to inhale sharply.

Ignoring my throbbing nipples, I gently caressed my belly before moving on to wash between my legs, which made me breathe quickly. The sensation was overwhelming, and I couldn't help but let out a small moan of pleasure.

I'd managed to awaken my sexual desire without meaning to. I'd ignored it during the past week because of my "no sex before the wedding" idea. It was a stupid decision, and I was stunned when Michael agreed.

I tried to concentrate on washing my thighs, but my hands had a mind of their own and kept moving toward my pussy.

A quick flick to my clit made my legs quiver with need, but I refused to take the final step of entering my core. I slid my hands back up my stomach, cupping my breasts and rubbing my nipples with my thumbs.

I groaned. "Why the hell did Michael agree to no sex for a week? We're both crazy."

I quickly turned the water off and reached out to grab a towel to dry off with. I wrapped a dry towel around my body and walked into the bedroom.

Standing in front of my wedding dress, hanging from the closet door, I felt tears of happiness prick my eyes. It was my wedding day! For some reason, it felt like a dream. I expected to wake up alone and without Michael at any second. Wiping the tears away, I knew my thoughts were silly. My love for Michael could endure anything.

My dress had very little shape on the hanger, but the A-line style would look beautiful on my full figure. The strapless bodice was layered with thin gauze and beautiful embroidered flowers that trailed from the back over the curve of my breasts.

I wasn't initially sure about the style because of my large breasts, but seeing Michael's mom in tears when I caught sight of her while trying it on at the bridal boutique made my decision.

Michael was going to be stunned when he saw me walking down the aisle toward him. His eyes always lit up when I entered a room he was in, but nothing could have prepared him for how I planned to look that afternoon.

I was going to become Mrs. Michael McKenzie, and I couldn't wait for him to slip the ring on my finger.

All of Michael's brothers and his parents had welcomed me into their family with open arms. For the first time since losing my own parents, I felt as though I had a family. It made me feel warm and fuzzy inside.

Smiling, I let the towel drop as I slipped my legs into a pair of panties, followed by a bra. Sometimes I wished my breasts were small enough to go without a bra, but no such luck.

After smoothing a sundress over my curves, I took a seat at the dressing table and brushed my long, dark curls before securing them on top of my head with a clip.

I'd just finished applying moisturizer to my face when my phone beeped with an incoming text message.

Are you feeling okay?

My smile deepened. Despite all the things to worry about today, Michael was still concerned about my well-being. He was always texting me. No matter where he was or who he was with, he would pick up his phone and send me a text to make sure I was okay.

I felt so much love for him.

I love you <3

I love you too, but that doesn't answer my question.

I chuckled. I could see him typing on his phone,

ready to leap into action if I showed any sign of discomfort. My heart swelled with joy, and I felt like I was going to burst from my love for him. Excitement coursed through my veins as I thought about the day ahead. I placed one hand on my stomach, over the growing love inside me, and typed my reply.

I feel wonderful and can't wait to become your wife.

Your love makes me a better person… I'm hard as rock talking to you.

The phone buzzed with an urgency that I was sure Michael was feeling. Michael's statement brought to mind some dirty thoughts, and I burst out laughing.

I'll take care of that later.

I have cum dripping from the head.

Moaning to myself, I fidgeted in the chair, trying to ease the pain that hadn't gone away since the shower. I needed him and didn't know how I'd make it through the wedding.

NO touching cock – that's mine.

As I typed the message, a soft knock sounded at the door. Oh no! I thought to myself as I walked to the bedroom door and opened it. Standing in the hallway were Pippa, Michael's mom, and Sebastian, who was carrying a tray of food. The smell of freshly brewed decaf coffee drifted toward me, and I smiled in appreciation as Sebastian carried the tray to the coffee table and set it down. With his task done, he settled into the only comfortable chair in the room. A huge, sexy grin spread across his face.

"Sebastian! You weren't raised in a barn. Let Lily sit down."

He winked at me. "Yes, ma'am." He stood and took my arm, guiding me into the seat with suppressed laughter lighting his eyes.

Pippa dragged a chair from in front of the dressing table to sit with me, and Sebastian lay down on the bed.

Having momentarily forgotten about my last message to Michael, I glanced at the phone I was still holding to see if he had replied.

What should I do with all this leaking cum?

I'd put my mouth on you if I was there
and clean it up…Use a towel, but do
not cum!

I was still looking at the phone when I blushed a lovely shade of red. I glanced up when Sebastian roared with laughter.

"Some message," he smirked.

"Sebastian, don't you have something better to do than embarrass Lily?" Pippa asked, not quite managing to hide the amusement in her voice.

Sebastian was handsome, with perfect features. His raven-black hair fell onto his forehead, contrasting with his suntanned skin. His square jaw was lightly dusted with yesterday's growth, and his dark eyes flashed with amusement. His long eyelashes and high cheekbones were the envy of any girl. He moved from his spot on the bed, his tight body moving with the fluidity of a panther, his muscles sleek and well-defined. He was breathtaking, but despite his raw, animal appeal, he had nothing on Michael.

"I'm not the one who embarrassed Lily. I'll leave you two alone and find Michael," Sebastian announced. As he was about to close the door behind him, he popped his head back in and looked at me.

"Don't forget to check if Michael replied," he said seriously.

I blushed even more as his mom shooed him away. I could still hear his laughter echoing down the hall, even through the closed door.

MICHAEL

THANKS TO THE HARDNESS IN MY JEANS, IT TOOK ME some time to leave my room after texting Lily.

Once I was presentable again, I made my way to the kitchen to eat breakfast with my dad and brothers. Mom had gone upstairs to be with Lily.

My father was quiet and brooding, which wasn't uncharacteristic; he was known as "a man of few words." After he finished eating, Dad cleared his throat and told me how proud he was of the man I'd become. He said he looked forward to welcoming Lily into the McKenzie family. After speaking, Dad made a quick exit, leaving his sons speechless in the kitchen.

That had been about four hours ago, before I took

another shower and dressed in a dark gray morning suit with a lilac cravat to match Sylvia's bridesmaid dress—or so Lily told me.

I wore a lilac and silver waistcoat on top of a crisp white shirt. Mom insisted on pressing my trousers again because she'd noticed a wrinkle in the front, much to my amusement.

It brought back childhood memories of being dressed in neatly pressed clothes for church and of Dad glaring at me and my brothers. We had been made to sit in a line on the two sofas in the living room while waiting for Mom to come downstairs so we could leave. No one dared to move with our father on guard.

Shaking my head at the memory, I sat on the edge of the bed, put on my boots, and moved to stand in front of the full-length mirror. I put on the jacket and looked at myself. Not bad. Not bad at all.

My six-foot, muscular frame filled out the suit perfectly. All I needed was a boutonniere to complete the look.

I turned at the sound of someone knocking on the door and shouted, "Come in."

Mom came through the door as though frightened

of what she might find. When her gaze fell on me, however, she burst into tears.

Stunned, I walked over to her and tried to wrap my arms around her, but she pushed me away.

"I'll mess up your jacket," she said, sniffling into the tissue I handed her.

"Mom, come and sit down." I tried to lead her to the chair by the window, but she slipped her arm free from mine.

"Oh, I'm fine. It's just seeing you dressed up like that, knowing you're about to officially make Lily part of this family as your wife." She continued to sniffle. "I can't believe one of my sons is about to get married."

Realizing that Mom needed to get things off her chest, I sat on the edge of the bed and waited, wondering what she was about to say next.

"My only hope is that your brothers start acting like grown-ups and find someone nice to settle down with instead of acting like manwhores," she said. Well, I hadn't expected that.

I looked stunned for a second before bursting out laughing at her description of my brothers. It was spot-on but hilarious coming out of her mouth.

I leaned over and grabbed a couple of tissues to

wipe my tears of laughter away. "Mom, no one is as bad as Sebastian. Besides, Ramon has a girlfriend," I told her, taking a drink of water and wishing it were whiskey to calm my nerves.

Mom slid into the chair she'd ignored earlier and gazed out the window. "Ramon's girlfriend is named Carla. I've only met her once or twice, but she seems lovely. I'm just not sure Ramon's that keen. We'll see. As for Sebastian, it's a wonder his tinkle hasn't fallen off from overuse."

I choked on the sip of water I'd just taken. Tinkle! What the fuck? "Have you been drinking?" I spluttered.

Mom rolled her eyes. "Really, Michael? Would you like me to rephrase it?"

I jumped to my feet and waved my hands in front of her. "No, the first time was enough," I said with a laugh. I wondered why Mom would suddenly say something so personal.

"Sit back down. I promise to behave," she admonished, just as someone knocked on the door.

"It's open," I shouted, taking my seat on the bed again as I watched Sebastian come through the door, half-dressed.

"What did I miss?" he asked.

I winked at Mom and smirked at Sebastian, who narrowed his eyes. "Mom was saying she couldn't understand why your 'tinkle' hadn't fallen off from overuse."

Sebastian stopped in his tracks, his face turning dark red as he sputtered, clearly at a loss for words. Well, that was a first. I mused.

I watched Sebastian struggle for a reply, his face growing redder with each passing second. I tried to hide my smile, but I couldn't. It was too damn amusing.

Coughing, Sebastian glared my way before ignoring me and turning to Mom. "Dad's looking for you. He's having trouble with his neck thing."

"Heck, there go my five minutes with your brother," she said as she stood and smoothed an imaginary wrinkle from her dress. As she reached the door, she turned back to the room and gave each of us a pointed stare. "I can't wait for the day when all my sons are married with babies. A house full of grandchildren," she finished with delight.

I grinned, and my grin widened when I saw my brother's pale complexion.

Just as she was about to close the door, Mom turned back and narrowed her eyes at Sebastian. "I also expect my grandchildren's mother to have a wedding ring on her finger. Preferably from one of my sons." With those words, she made a quick exit.

"What the hell has gotten into Mom?" Sebastian finally choked out. "I know before you hooked up with Lily, she was always talking about us getting married, your remarrying, and having grandkids, but, well, Tinkle?"

I burst into laughter just as my three remaining brothers walked into the room, looking mischievous.

As I looked through the bedroom window and watched some small children playing near the fountain, I thought back to breakfast with Pippa that morning. We had both decided to plan another wedding within the next twelve months. I wanted sisters. And I wanted more babies in the family so that mine and Michael's children would grow up with their cousins.

Lucien would be the most difficult, although I had plans where he was concerned. Ramon was dating Carla, and apparently had been for some time. He neglected to inform his mom, so that hadn't gone down too well when he first told her. Carla seemed really nice, a bit reserved, and not at all how I expected a girlfriend to behave toward her boyfriend. I first met Carla at the ranch about three Sundays ago. At first, whenever Ramon tried to kiss her, which hadn't been that often, Carla jumped as though it were unexpected. I sighed, wondering if they were the right fit. Maybe she didn't have feelings for Ramon, or maybe she was just shy around his family. Either way, something seemed off between them.

Sebastian seemed like a player, but I kept that opinion to myself. He needed a sweet woman. Someone who was so out of his league that he wouldn't know what to do about her. He needed someone who would ignore his flirting and make him chase her instead of the other way around.

I didn't know much about Ruben because he'd started keeping to himself. When I first met him, he flirted with me, and I thought he was fun. But something had recently changed him. He used to be open with his brothers and join in the skirmishes when they got a rugby ball. However, Ruben was never seen with a woman, and he seemed to spend all his time at his club, Kenza. The other day, I overheard Michael at the house commenting on his brother's lack of female companionship while Ruben was sitting outside with his brothers. Ruben said he hadn't had time because of the new business. He then changed the subject, obviously wanting to draw attention away from himself.

Suddenly brought back to the present by Sylvia's screech, I blinked rapidly and stared at the McKenzie brothers' receptionist. She'd become a good friend of mine over the past month. My friend Sabrina from high school should be at the wedding as well, but she's been delayed in England.

"Lily, you look gorgeous! I cannot wait to see Michael's reaction. He's a big softie with you," Sylvia said, slowly turning me around for a better view. "I love the floral detail on the bodice." She smoothed her hand over the flowers while I looked her over. She was always dressed in beautiful clothes, and her makeup was always flawless. No matter how busy or harassed she was at her desk at McKenzie's, her appearance never faltered. Today, though, she seemed to glow from within, and I didn't think she'd be the only one to notice.

"You don't look so bad yourself. Some of those McKenzie brothers are going to do some drooling of their own when they see you in that dress," I said, grinning as I watched the blush work its way up Sylvia's face.

She was wearing a lavender A-line dress with a strapless bodice that showed off her slender figure. The hairdresser had swept her blonde hair up and secured it to the top of her head with jeweled clips. She looked older than twenty-three, although she usually looked seventeen. The blush she displayed when I mentioned the McKenzie brothers made me wonder if she had her eye on one of them.

"Lily, stop switching off," Sylvia admonished.

"Sorry." I took a deep breath and moved to stand in front of the mirror that had been brought into the room for me.

"I actually came to tell you that we have about five minutes before we have to head downstairs. I think Lucien is waiting for us at the bottom of the stairs."

"Oh boy. Okay, let's do this," I said, smoothing my hand over my stomach, which was full of butterflies.

Sylvia opened the door and led me toward the stairs to meet Lucien.

Despite being Michael's brother, I had felt an instant connection to Lucien. He was the brother I never had, so it made sense that he would give me away. He choked up when I asked him to walk me down the aisle. After he came back down to earth, Lucien tried to talk me out of it. He said it would draw more attention to himself, which he had been avoiding since the accident. I dragged him down to the sofa with me and eventually received his tentative acceptance.

The thing was, although he was scarred, it wasn't as bad as he thought, at least the visible part. The scarring started on his right cheek and traveled down his neck and underneath his clothing, which I hadn't seen.

Once he realized that I really wanted him by my side on the big day, he accepted and threw himself into helping organize the wedding with his mom.

I tried to pull myself together because I was always upset when I thought about what Lucien lost because of the accident. There he was, standing at the bottom of the stairs, watching me walk down.

"Gorgeous. My brother is a very lucky man, as he knows," Lucien stated, grinning.

The whole house had been decorated with ribbons and flowers while I was upstairs with Sylvia getting ready.

Lucien took my hand, brought it up to his lips, and placed a gentle kiss on it. Then he wrapped his arm around me and held his arm out to Sylvia. He escorted both of us outside.

I stopped short as I took in the transformed ranch. Marquees for the reception and dancing had been set up to one side of the barn, which had also been decorated with lilac, pink, and white ribbons. The ribbons transformed everything from the house to the paddocks close to the house. The horses had been moved to the far pastures so they wouldn't be spooked by all the people.

The transformation was amazing and brought tears to my eyes.

"You ready?" Lucien asked.

"Yes, I am." I turned to look at him and saw him shift slightly. His nerves were clear in the way his fingers clenched together and his gaze darted everywhere but up. I knew he was trying to hide it from me, and that he was willing to suffer through this for me. That knowledge brought tears to my eyes. "Lucien, thank you for doing this for me," I said, my voice cracking slightly from the emotion welling up in my throat. I felt loved by everyone in my new family. "I know you'd rather not, but it means a lot to me. I couldn't think of anyone else I'd rather have walk me down the aisle."

Lucien opened his mouth to speak, but nothing came out.

"I'll wait over there," Sylvia interrupted, putting some distance between them.

I had momentarily forgotten that Sylvia was walking with us.

"Lily, I love you."

My eyes opened wide in shock, causing Lucien to laugh and flash his gorgeous smile.

"I love you like a sister, Lily. You've made my brother a pussy, but we won't get into that today."

Lucien's laughter deepened as I swatted him on the arm. "There isn't much I wouldn't do for you. I hope you know that. If Michael screws up again—although I think he's learned his lesson—don't hesitate to come to me. I'll always be there for you. Considering how we've been teasing Michael all day, I think we should get going."

5

MICHAEL

STANDING WITH THREE OF MY BROTHERS IN FRONT OF everyone, waiting for Lily to arrive on Lucien's arm, was nerve-racking. My brothers spent the morning telling me that Lily had probably snuck away or, even worse, run off with Lucien, which didn't help.

I'd finally come to terms with my possessiveness toward Lily and accepted that she was one of my brother's best friends. It hadn't been easy, and every now and then, I had to stop myself from making a comment. Lily found this amusing and would plant a hot kiss on my lips before disappearing with Lucien for coffee.

Glancing around, I saw my family, friends, and McKenzie Holdings employees smiling in my direction, glancing quickly toward the back to see if Lily had arrived.

She didn't have far to walk as she was arriving from the house where we'd both spent the night in separate rooms. It had been difficult, as I had never slept apart from Lily for a month before, but I managed.

Sebastian nudged me, causing me to look at his brother, who was looking toward the back of the seats.

I followed his gaze, and my breath stopped while my heart started beating wildly in my chest.

"Breathe, Michael," Ramon whispered in my ear.

I exhaled, having held my breath at the sight of Lily. I watched her walk down the aisle on my brother's arm.

She never once moved her gaze from me as she glided closer, a slight smile on her lips and her eyes bright as the sun.

She was the most beautiful woman I had ever seen when she stopped beside me. Lucien took my hand, kissed her knuckles, and placed her hand in mine. He gave me a serious look, then stepped back to stand beside me and our brothers.

"Breathtaking," I whispered to Lily before leaning

in and kissing her softly. "I missed you," I said against her lips, finding it difficult to pull away.

Lily smiled, caressing my face with one hand, and pulled back when Sebastian started coughing loudly. After hearing a few snickers in the background, Lily and I smiled at each other before turning to face the front so that we could be married. The whole wedding seemed to pass in a blur. One minute, we were exchanging rings, and the next, I was asked to kiss the bride—which, of course, I had no problem with.

The moment my lips met Lily's, I forgot about everyone and everything else as I tasted my woman, my wife. The sound of cheers and annoying wolf whistles, obviously from my brothers, pulled me from Lily's embrace and into the present.

I moved a breath away from Lily and caressed her face. "Hello, wife," I said, grinning.

"Hello, husband," Lily replied, reaching up for another toe-curling kiss.

"Okay, you two. That's enough. There are four bachelors here," Sebastian stated dryly.

"Not if Mom has her way," I smirked, ignoring him as I took Lily's arm and led her back down the aisle. I couldn't wipe the grin off my face.

"Ramon's next," Ruben commented behind us, which made me chuckle. He continued escorting Sylvia down the aisle, and I caught him struggling not to gawk at her cleavage. Each time she took a step, her breasts looked ready to spill out of her bodice.

Ramon snickered beside Ruben. "Nope, but it might be you if you keep looking at what you're looking at."

Ruben turned and glared at him before glancing back at Sylvia to make sure she hadn't heard their conversation.

"Jailbait," Sebastian whispered as Ramon chuckled and patted Ruben on the shoulder.

AFTER WHAT FELT LIKE HOURS OF TAKING PICTURES with family and friends, I took the beer that George had given me and stood looking at my friend, who was also my driver.

He looked much better since I made him rest. He'd had three nurses; the last one had lasted the longest because she could hold her own, and Janet had said something to him about his manners or rather his nurse problem. He'd finally hooked up with Janet, who was also a guest of George's at the wedding.

"I don't think I've ever seen you this happy," George finally commented.

I took a long drag of the beer before turning to watch Lily talking to Mom and Sylvia.

"That's because I haven't been this happy before. She makes me whole." I laughed in embarrassment. "What about you and Janet? You two seem rather friendly," I said, trying to change the subject.

"We're fine," he replied, turning red. "Lily's on her way over," he said with relief. "I'd better go find Janet."

I laughed as he darted away toward the dancing marquee with a free bar. The meal would be served soon, and my stomach was growling in anticipation. I hadn't been able to finish breakfast thanks to my nerves.

Lily approached with a wicked grin on her face. She was up to something. I held my arms open, and she walked straight into them, wrapping her arms tightly around my waist.

We stood silently, holding each other, before Lily said, "I've missed being close to you. If I ever suggest going without sex again, please promise me you won't agree."

"I promise." I leaned forward and kissed the top of her head, smiling softly.

"We haven't cuddled in bed with skin-to-skin contact like we used to because we've both been afraid of breaking my rule. I was an idiot. My body craves being close to you and having you inside me."

Groaning, I clenched my jaw, breathing heavily against Lily. My blood heated for this woman. My wife. "Lily, I'm sure you can feel what you're doing to me," I moaned. Lily rubbed against my erection while my hand traveled south and landed on her bottom.

I heard her breathing change, so I decided to tease her and come clean. "I woke up coming on my stomach this morning."

She froze. "What?"

"I dreamed about that time you rode me on the Harley. I woke up shooting cum all over my stomach. It was the hottest dream I've ever had." I imagined crawling under her dress and moving her thong to the side. I would then slide my fingers along her wet lips, then slid two fingers inside her.

"Michael," Lily panted, pressing closer. "You can't tell me things like that when we're surrounded by family and friends! And what the hell were you thinking about to get all throbbing?"

"I was thinking about crawling under your dress, putting my mouth on you, and putting my fingers in you."

Taking a steadying breath, I shifted slightly to create more space between us. I needed to calm down before I came like a teenager. She always made my body react that way. I was amazed that I ever lasted long enough to get my cock inside her and get her pregnant because, with just one look from her, I was hard as hell, and with just one touch, I was ready to come.

Ruben brought us out of our wicked thoughts by coughing once or twice to get our attention.

"Mom ordered me to come get you before you missed your own reception," he said with a smirk as he started walking back to the marquee. Then, he changed course to intercept one of his servers.

I groaned and gave Lily a quick kiss. My fingers slid down her arm, raising gooseflesh on her skin, before I took her hand. "Let's go celebrate with everyone. We can have our own celebration later. When I have you all to myself."

As Lily started to move away from me, I wanted nothing more than to pull her back into my arms.

6

LILY

A FEW HOURS AGO, THE HAPPIEST DAY OF MY LIFE HAD taken place. I had become Mrs. Michael McKenzie in a beautiful ceremony at Michael's parents' ranch.

I'd seen Michael in suits regularly, but I'd never seen him look so handsome in the suit he wore today. He took my breath away. His brothers looked just as handsome in the same type of suit, but they wore different colored cravats with matching waistcoats.

I gave Sebastian a pink one, Lucien a pale blue one, Ramon a lemon one, Ruben a pale green one, and their father, Elias, a deep purple one. They all looked handsome standing together for the "father and sons" photograph, which I had insisted on.

We dined on a beautiful meal. The starter was

41

chicken parmesan crostini, which whet everyone's appetite. This was followed by slow-roasted, herb-crusted beef tenderloin. Dessert was a decadent chocolate mousse with fresh raspberries — the perfect way to top it all off.

I hadn't realized just how hungry I was until the food was placed in front of me. My stomach felt like there were four babies inside instead of two.

I went outside to the patio, hoping Michael would follow me so I could tell him about the twins. I had put it off because of the stress I felt he was under in the lead-up to the wedding, but I didn't want to wait any longer.

"Hey, beautiful."

"Hey, Sebastian, you look handsome," I replied, giving him a hug. He really did. I'd noticed some of the female guests drooling over him. With his jacket off, you could see how tight his abs were, which I was sure he knew.

"You eyeing me up?" he asked, grinning.

"I am." I smirked. "I'm trying to decide who I need to introduce you to." I grinned mischievously, my smile deepening at the sour look on his face.

"No, you're not going to introduce me to—" he trailed off, "—her."

I looked across the way to see why he had stopped talking, and I saw that he had been knocked sideways by Ramon's date. "Ah, Sebastian."

"Who's she here with?" he asked, still stunned. "Lily, who is that bodacious babe with?"

I snickered. "You did not just call her a bodacious babe?" How old are you? Seventeen!"

Trust me, no horny seventeen-year-old boy would think of doing what I'm thinking of doing to her."

"Bodacious!" I giggled, still unable to recover from his use of the word.

"Bill and Ted's," Sebastian replied, not really listening to me.

"What?"

"Never mind. You haven't said who she's with."

Crap. He was really taken with her. This wasn't going to go down well. "You need to keep your zipper up. She's here with Ramon."

I heard a laugh behind us.

7

MICHAEL

Keep your zipper up! What was Lily discussing with Sebastian? Then, I noticed the woman he couldn't take his eyes from—Ramon's girlfriend.

"How can she be with Ramon?" Sebastian asked, frowning.

I pulled my wife close and laughed at Seb. "Well, I guess our brother is finally serious about someone, and Lucien needs to get his facts straight in the future."

"She can't be with him. Are you sure?"

I frowned. I'd never seen Seb upset about a woman being with someone else before. He usually just moved on.

"I'm sorry, but she is," Lily told him.

She was walking toward us, and Sebastian couldn't stop staring.

"Hey, Lily. Do you know where Ramon is?" Carla asked.

"I haven't seen Ramon in a while." Lily looked at me for help. I noticed, but I couldn't move my gaze from my brother. Oh, what the hell. "Let me introduce you to Sebastian, our brother. Sebastian, this is Carla."

He stood there frozen while exchanging heated looks with Carla until Lily nudged him.

"Carla, it's a pleasure to meet you." He took her hand and held it. She seemed just as taken. "Are you really with Ramon?"

This question seemed to bring her back to her senses, and she pulled her hand away as though it had been burned. "It's great to meet you, but I'd better go find Ramon." She turned around and headed back toward the marquee.

"I need some fresh air," Sebastian murmured before heading off in the direction of the garage. He was obviously unaware that he was already outside.

Lily turned and wrapped her arms around me before snuggling close.

"Are you getting tired, Lily?" I moved my hand up

and down in a soft caress over my wife's back and the curve of her hip. "We can leave if you're ready," I said, hoping she was.

I'd had an amazing day, but after the long day of festivities, all I wanted was to take my wife back to the hotel's honeymoon suite so I could make love to her.

"Soon, Michael. Soon." Lily met my gaze. "I love you, Michael. I'm so glad you married me today because I have something to tell you. You can't get away from me now."

What the hell? This couldn't be good. "Do I really want to know this?"

"Oh, yes."

"Well, get on with it! You're killing me."

"We're having twins."

8

LILY

THE MINUTE I SAID, "WE'RE HAVING TWINS," I watched Michael's face lose all color.

"Twins?" he stuttered, taking a step back. He fell into one of the patio chairs when it touched the back of his knees. "Are you sure?"

I held back a smile, knowing he wouldn't appreciate it at that moment. "Yes, I'm sure. After the sonogram, you went outside the room to call your mom. The doctor told me to buy two of everything."

He ran his hands over his face. "Why didn't she wait until I was back in the room to tell us?" he asked, sounding puzzled.

I walked over to Michael and perched on his lap,

49

his arms going around my waist and mine around his neck.

"She probably didn't want you passing out."

He opened and closed his mouth, but nothing came out. I never thought I'd see the day when he was left speechless.

"Hey, I've been looking for you two," Lucien said, walking up the steps to the porch. He frowned when he saw Michael's face. "What's wrong? You can't have messed up already, especially with Lily still sitting on your lap."

"Twins," Michael announced.

"Twins," Lucien repeated, still not understanding until Michael rubbed my belly.

Lucien met my gaze, and the minute he realized what we were talking about, his eyes widened. "Twins! As in, two babies! Good God! Does Mom know?"

"No, I just told Michael." I snuggled into Michael, who was starting to get some color back in his cheeks.

"I like babies. Two is good. That means I can have one," Lucien said, grinning like an idiot.

Lucien and I stared at Michael, waiting for his reaction. There wasn't one. Michael returned

Lucien's grin, kissed me briefly on the lips, and helped me to my feet.

"You, my brother, can go find your own woman," Michael told him.

I rolled my eyes and walked over to Lucien, giving him a hug as his hand crept down and landed on my butt. I pulled away and smacked the back of his head. "Stop trying to get a reaction from him."

"Why isn't it working?" Lucien frowned.

"It's not working, brother, because I've finally realized that you two really do look at each other as brother and sister. So I have nothing to worry about. Plus, I trust Lily. And you," Michael said, pulling me into his arms. "I should have trusted you both from the beginning, and I regret that."

Lucien stood in front of us, shaking his head. He was obviously still in shock at our announcement. He needed someone to build a relationship with. He needed someone who wouldn't flinch at his scars. I had someone in mind. Unfortunately, Sabrina was pretty strong-willed and against relationships, but I'd see what I could do.

"Lily, where'd you go?" Lucien asked.

I gave him the smile I used to get what I wanted. Up to now, Lucien hadn't been able to resist it. I said,

"I was just thinking about the kind of woman you need."

His eyes widened in shock. "Now, Lily, we've been through this before."

Ignoring him, I continued, counting the points on her fingers: "She'd have to be strong-willed because you're a pain in the ass at times. She'd have to have curves and a great personality." I paused to consider whether to speak the next part aloud. What the heck. "She'd have to have a lot of stamina, considering you haven't had sex in ages."

I grinned as he gave me the evil eye. I felt Michael go still against me.

"I need a drink," Lucien mumbled.

He turned and shook his head as he followed the path to the bar.

"You, my gorgeous wife, are going to get in trouble one of these days for teasing Lucien."

Michael caressed my face and placed a gentle kiss on my lips. "You taste good. I can't wait until later," he whispered. He moved his lips to nibble my earlobe, then moved down my neck to my collarbone.

I tilted my head to one side to give him better access. "Mmm, me either. I can't wait for you to see my underwear—or lack thereof."

Michael's mouth stilled against my neck. "Explain, lack of."

I kissed his neck and slipped my hands inside his jacket, moving them down his back. I felt his cock go rigid against me when I squeezed his butt. "I only have a lacy garter on under the dress."

His cock surged against my stomach. "Are you telling me that you have a naked pussy under this dress?"

"Yes," I whispered, rubbing against his shaft.

Michael grabbed my hips and thrust against me.

"I need to touch you. I need to feel how wet you are."

I groaned because there was nowhere for us to go —at least not yet. "We can't leave. Not yet. Your mom wouldn't be happy if we did."

Michael grabbed my hips to hold me still while he moved against me. "I'd be happy."

I was wet and aching for his touch between my legs. Before I became pregnant, I craved him. Now, I couldn't get enough of him. One touch from Michael, and I was ready to climax.

"Let me touch you," he said as he lifted the front of my dress, which was trapped between us.

"Michael, there you are."

He growled in my ear, trying to control his breathing as his mom approached.

"That's what you get for being impatient," I whispered.

He wasn't the only one who was frustrated, though.

9

MICHAEL

She would never change. Growing up with my brothers, she was the ultimate cock blocker. She seemed to have a "hanky-panky" antenna, and the minute one of us had a girl over and was about to get lucky, she'd appear. She'd always shout first to give us a warning, but it was still damn embarrassing, no matter how old we were.

Lily stood in front of me, shielding my body part from view. We both turned and watched as Mom approached with a knowing look on her face.

"Michael, for goodness' sake! You're not a horny teenager sneaking around, waiting for me to find you anymore. You'll be able to get to Lily shortly, but first,

55

you need to go in there and have a slow dance before everyone starts to leave."

At Mom's comment, I felt Lily shake with silent laughter. Her face was buried in my chest. At the same time, I caught Ruben snickering.

"You boys! I know what sex is. How else do you think you and your brothers were born?" She shook her head and started walking toward the marquee, which had been set up for dancing. "Five minutes," she shouted back.

"Did Mom just mention sex?" Ruben asked, sitting down and looking rather pale.

"Oh, please." Lily pushed away and glared at Ruben and me. "Your mom and dad probably had sex in all the places you five used to disappear to."

Ruben stood up, shuddered, and gave his attention to Lily. "I really did not need that image in my head," he said. He walked off toward one of the servers from his club.

I took Lily's hand and started leading her toward the marquee. But first, I caught Ruben and Rosie, his server, practically nose-to-nose, arguing.

Ruben's club, Kenza, had been closed for the past week while the front windows and frames were replaced due to vandalism, leaving everyone stunned and angry. The attack felt personal, but out of the five of us, Ruben was the one who would go out of his way to avoid trouble. Once upon a time, he would have been in the thick of it. When he found out who was responsible, there would be hell to pay.

Because of the attack on Kenza, though, Ruben's staff had been given paid leave and asked to work at the wedding. I was curious about Rosie, whom Ruben had trouble staying away from. His preoccupation with her had been hard to miss, even for me, distracted as I was by my wife's beauty.

My wife. I didn't think I'd ever tire of calling her that. As I walked up the aisle toward her, she took my breath away and nearly brought me to tears. Lily was not only beautiful on the outside, but on the inside as well, and she wanted to spend her life with me. She had me wrapped around her little finger, as all my brothers knew and joked about. They could joke, but I knew that if they had the same chance at happiness that I did, they'd be the same way. I couldn't wait to see it.

However, Lily mentioning that she had someone in mind for Lucien didn't sit well with me. My brother had deep scars, which were much deeper inside than the ones visible on his body. I couldn't imagine what it must have been like for him to have the fire burn into his skin while he was trying to help accident victims. Since then, he'd closed himself off from the world and from women. He indulged Lily, but throwing women at him was something else entirely. I just hoped Lucien wouldn't disappoint Lily too much.

We entered the marquee where the band had set up for the evening and walked straight onto the dance floor. I pulled Lily into my arms, squeezing her tightly.

The singer announced that it was the last dance of the evening and started singing "I Don't Want to Miss a Thing," a slow, romantic song originally by Aerosmith.

As I slowly moved Lily around the dance floor, I spotted my brother, Sebastian, standing a bit too close to Ramon's girlfriend. I hadn't missed the instant attraction that had flown between them not too long ago on the patio. But what the hell was Sebastian doing?

Lily noticed me frowning. "Michael, it might be best if you don't get involved."

"There's something funny going on."

Lily frowned up at me, raising an eyebrow in question.

"I don't mean with Sebastian. I mean between Carla and Ramon. They just don't seem like a couple."

"You mean they don't seem attracted to each other?" Lily finished for me.

"Yeah." I tucked her head back into my shoulder and whispered, "I've never seen Ramon give her a passionate kiss. I've seen them hug and kiss, but never passionately."

"Speaking of passion, how about showing me some?" she purred.

I grinned. "I don't think Mom would approve of me showing you passion on the dance floor, but I'm sure you can feel what you do to me."

She rubbed against my throbbing shaft ever so slightly. I had been hard as stone since the porch when she announced that she wasn't wearing panties. I couldn't wait to be alone with her in the hotel room.

When the music stopped, I held on to Lily, but she raised her head to look at me. "Let's go. I need you inside me."

I growled and practically dragged her toward the entrance of the marquee. She didn't need to be told twice.

10

LILY

GEORGE HAD WANTED TO DRIVE US TO THE HOTEL, BUT he eventually gave in when Janet said she wanted to spend more time with him. It was endearing to watch their romance blossom, from George blushing whenever Janet touched his arm to the heated looks that passed between them. Lily didn't think they were having monkey sex, but they were certainly doing it quite often.

The limousine was the typical wedding vehicle—a long, black stretch limo with blacked-out windows and a privacy partition between the driver and the passengers. The added privacy put all sorts of wicked thoughts in my head.

Michael was sitting back in the seat with his arm

around me. My cheek rested against his chest. Looking down, I saw how aroused he was. His thick, long cock looked ready to burst the zipper. I licked my lips in anticipation as my sex contracted. I was so sensitive since becoming pregnant.

The sex between us had become more sedate since he began reading all the baby books, which was driving me insane. I had plans for our wedding night, and sedate wasn't one of them.

I moved my hand and slid it into his pants, freeing the zipper as I did. I slowly trailed my finger from the tip to the base. I felt him shudder as his heart started to race. I rubbed my hand along his length, then scraped my nails over his balls and worked my way up his cock to the tip. I didn't think it was possible, but he grew even more with my touch, until he was throbbing in my hand.

I took my eyes off his twitching shaft and looked up at Michael. He had his head resting against the back of the seat and was watching me through half-closed eyes. I grinned and slipped onto the floor of the vehicle between his legs. Leaning in, I took him into my mouth. I felt his hands thread through my hair as he let out a low groan of pleasure. The sound spurred me on, and I became eager to see how far I could push him to the edge. As I continued, Michael's grip on my hair tightened, and his breath quickened. I felt his body tense beneath me—a sure sign that he was close to reaching his peak. With a mischievous glint in my eye, I let him slide free of my mouth. He let out a frustrated growl. I could tell he was desperate for release, but I wanted to tease him a little longer. I wanted to make him beg for it.

My clit throbbed; if I had been wearing panties, they would have been soaked. I had to stop myself from rubbing my thighs together for relief. I slid his pants down, giving his cock and balls more freedom from the tight fabric. Michael's cock jerked at the sensation of my breath, and he groaned as I exhaled slowly. He arched his hips, wanting my mouth. I gave in to his desire, taking him into my mouth and feeling him pulse with pleasure before letting him slip free once again.

I gave him a wicked smile before wrapping my hand around him. He was long and thick, pulsating with need. His mushroom-shaped head was darker than the rest of his cock, and pre-cum oozed from the slit. I swiped it off with my tongue and felt Michael's legs quiver.

I softly scraped from the tip to the root with a

manicured fingernail, which made him twitch and clench his fists at his sides.

Wanting more access, I dragged his pants and briefs down his legs. He kicked his shoes off, and I tugged the pants and briefs free. His body was now completely exposed and vulnerable.

Kneeling between his thighs, I turned my back to him and asked, "Unzip me?"

"Lily, you're killing me."

"I know."

My wedding dress fell from me, pooling around my legs and leaving me naked. Over the past couple of weeks, my breasts had grown, and because I was having twins, my stomach had already started to expand. Michael found my changing shape sexy as hell, but he held back. He wouldn't stand a chance tonight. I twisted around to face him again and heard his breath catch.

"Have you really been naked under there all day?"

I grinned, bent my head, and licked him from balls to tip. Then, I swirled my tongue around the head. I sucked him into my mouth and massaged the crown with my tongue.

Michael put his hands on my head and held me in place, but I had other ideas. With one powerful suck, his cock touched the back of my throat. He cursed and arched closer, making me wetter for his touch.

After one final swipe of my tongue around the head, I licked down to the base of his penis and massaged his balls with my mouth. When I felt he was close, I released him, licked back up to the tip, and moved up toward his chest. I smoothed my hands over his abs under his shirt and rubbed around his nipples. His shirt restricted me, so I quickly undid the buttons before spreading the shirt wide open to revel in his naked body.

As I licked and nibbled at his nipples, his cock swelled even more and nestled between my breasts. The thickness between my breasts had me rocking back and forth in ecstasy. His body trembled as I caressed his balls, and his dick was squished between my breasts. His moans grew louder, signaling his impending release.

Michael started to caress my shoulder, which was the only place he could reach. But I needed his hands on my breasts and his cock inside me. I rose from the floor of the car and sat astride him.

"I love you, Mrs. McKenzie," he said, caressing my hips and slowly moving one hand over my stomach.

His touch brought tears to my eyes every time, with our babies snuggled inside.

Leaning forward, I brought our mouths together in a slow, sweet, seductive kiss. The lips of my sex opened along his length as he glided back and forth through my wet heat.

"Fuck, Lily."

11

MICHAEL

LILY WAS SO AROUSING THAT I WAS AFRAID I'D CLIMAX before entering her. She had always been perfect to me, inside and out. But since she'd become pregnant, her body had started to change. Her breasts had grown larger, and her stomach had swelled slightly with his children. I was still astonished that such an amazing woman wanted me, but I wasn't going to doubt her anymore because I loved her with everything I had.

Feeling her wetness along my dick was driving me insane. The week of no sex had been excruciating. Despite our promises, we couldn't resist driving each other crazy with hot words, promises, and the occasional flash of flesh. I was damn frustrated, and she was lucky I hadn't grabbed her and taken her over the dinner table in front of my whole family.

Sitting up, she moved slightly backward, coating my balls with her wetness as she settled on them with my dick—a large, hot, weeping rod—between us.

"Hold my hips."

I reached out and steadied her as she took hold of my aching cock. After a few strokes, she lifted up and took the full length of me inside her.

The mere sight of her naked and aroused, sitting on top of me, was enough to send me over the edge. I clenched my jaw, trying to stave off my orgasm as she sat above me, unmoving. Thank God.

Lily stretched up to the roof of the limo, leaving me short of breath. She gripped my cock so tightly with her vaginal muscles. "Lily," I groaned.

"Hold onto my hips to keep me from falling."

I held her hips as she arched her back slightly, thrusting her breasts toward me.

"Lie back against the seat. I want you to watch me fuck you."

"Oh God." I leaned my head back against the seat and looked at my wife. Her breasts were swollen with deep rose-colored nipples hard as stone. I steadied her with one hand and massaged her breasts with the other. Since her pregnancy, her nipples had become extremely sensitive. All I had to do was pinch and suckle them for a few minutes, and she would climax without me stimulating her pussy at all.

I couldn't take my eyes off her body.

"You like it?" she asked.

"God, babe. You are so hot. I love how your body is changing."

She smirked. "Yeah, I bet you do. Bigger boobs."

I laughed, but it turned into a groan when she squeezed my dick. I wasn't sure how much more I could take. A week of abstinence had me on edge.

Lily moved her hands from the roof to her breasts and started to massage and pinch her nipples. She was a tease and knew how crazy it made me to watch her touch herself.

Growling, I held her hips tighter so I could thrust into her while watching her pleasure herself.

"Lily, I can't stop."

"Michael, come."

My balls pulled up and my cock grew just before I started coating her walls with hot semen. Lily started to climax around me. She writhed around on my oversensitive shaft, nearly sending me into another orgasm. Only with Lily!

Completely spent, she collapsed against me and wrapped her arms around my neck.

"I love you, my husband," she whispered into my neck.

"Mmm, I love you, too." I turned her face to the side so that I could kiss her. "You're amazing, but I think we should get dressed because we're about five minutes out."

Her eyes widened in shock. "I'd forgotten."

I put my hands on her hips again and lifted her off my cock, causing us to moan.

"Michael?" Lily asked, looking at my hardening dick.

"That's what happens when you ban sex," I replied, grinning. "Babe, just sit your sexy butt right here." I positioned her on the seat beside me while untangling my pants from her dress. I pulled up my pants and fastened them. Kneeling at my feet, I helped her slide her dress up her body. "It's a shame to cover you back up." I leaned forward and sucked one of her nipples into my mouth, massaging it with my tongue. She shuddered and broke out in goosebumps.

"Michael! You have to stop."

She arched into me as I moved to her other breast.

"Oh God, Michael, I'm so close."

Her breasts were sensitive, and I loved that I could bring her to orgasm by paying attention only to them. I lay gently against her stomach and continued sucking and nibbling one breast while lifting my hand to rub and pinch the other.

She gasped and shuddered as she climaxed in my arms. She clutched my head to her.

I gave her breasts a couple of licks before breathing heavily and pulling her dress further up to cover them with unsteady hands. Hearing her climax made my cock as hard as a spike.

"We're here," I whispered.

"I'm not sure I can move."

I gave her a wicked grin as I pulled her forward from the seat and helped her back into the dress.

"We're already checked into our room. Ruben stopped on his way to the wedding to take care of it," I told her, pulling the keycard for the suite out of my inside pocket.

"Thank goodness."

The chauffeur opened the door for us. I climbed out first, then turned to hold my hand out to his beautiful wife.

MICHAEL INSISTED ON CARRYING ME ALL THE WAY through the hotel to our suite on the top floor. If people were watching us, I didn't notice because my eyes never left my husband's.

I was surprised in the car when he let me initiate what happened in there. It was hot as hell and left me aching for more. As Michael had said, I'd banned sex, but I was certainly ready to lift the ban.

Once we were alone in our suite, Michael put me back on my feet. We spent the night in our suite before heading off on our honeymoon tomorrow.

As I looked around, I couldn't help but notice the abundance of flowers spread throughout, including lilies and roses, my two favorite flowers. I covered my mouth in surprise. Michael had done this for me. He was the most romantic man I'd ever known.

"Thank you," I whispered, looking at him before turning back to look at the rest of the room.

The room was decorated in creams and beiges, with matching furniture. A leather corner sofa sat on one side of the room, and a large flat-screen television took up wall space on the opposite side. There was a wet bar with four stools hidden underneath. To the right was a door that led to the bedroom, which I couldn't wait to get Michael into.

"It's beautiful, Michael," I gasped. I turned to look at him, only to find that his eyes were already fixed on me.

"You're the beautiful one, Lily." He paused, a touch of pain flashing through his eyes. "About tonight..."

I cut him off. "Oh, no, you don't. Tonight is my wedding night, and you are not going to hold back. I won't break. The doctor said sex is healthy during pregnancy, except toward the end, when your sperm could send me into labor." I finished with a smirk when I saw the horror on his face. He was so worried about my well-being and that of our future children that he would put himself through physical pain to refrain from having sex with me. That knowledge both comforted and excited me.

He needed a distraction, so I reached behind my dress, tugged the zipper down, and allowed the garment to pool around my feet. Stepping out of it in my heels, I bent over and gave him a direct view between my thighs as I picked up the dress. I turned around, fully naked except for the garter, and saw Michael's anguished expression turn hot as I sauntered toward the bedroom. I moved my hips slowly in a silky, inviting dance that captivated him. His gaze followed each stride I took.

I walked into the room and climbed onto the enormous bed. I struck a seductive pose in the middle of the bed, lying on my side with my arm on my hip, facing Michael, who stood in the doorway.

There was fire in Michael's eyes as they traveled up my body from my toes, lingering between my legs and intensifying the throbbing sensation. I urgently wanted him to touch me, but first, I needed to see him naked.

"Take your clothes off," I commanded, my voice thick with lust.

I didn't need to ask him twice. He stripped in

record time, but left one crucial item on. "Take off all your clothes."

Through my half-closed eyes, I watched him slowly remove his briefs. My mouth watered as he stood up straight with his cock fully erect. By the look of things, he was just as desperate as I was for more attention.

"Stroke yourself."

He paused and offered me a slight grin as he ran his palm from the crown to the root.

"Are you leaking?"

"Oh yeah."

"Do it again, but squeeze your balls this time."

I watched him repeat the process, his hand now massaging his balls. His dick throbbed and twitched. I could see pre-cum dribbling out of his slit. "That sight is incredibly hot."

"Fist your cock."

Seeing Michael touch himself turned me on so much, especially when he moved his hand back and forth. I took my hand off my hip and started rubbing my nipples. It felt so good that I couldn't help but scissor my legs, trying to relieve the tension.

"Fuck. I'm not going to be able to hold on if you keep doing that." His words came out in quick pants.

"Mmm, it feels good, Michael. I need you to make me come."

Before I could register what was happening, I was lying on my back with Michael's mouth between my legs. He parted me like a flower and ran his tongue back and forth between my folds.

"You're so wet, baby."

I groaned. "I need you."

"I know, but let me love you like this first. Keep touching your breasts. I'm leaving the garter on. It's sexy as hell."

With that, he sucked my clit into his mouth and inserted two fingers inside me. My orgasm hit. I shook uncontrollably, unable to stop coming. My insides contracted so tightly around his fingers that they felt enormous inside me. Michael didn't let up as I felt myself about to go off again. He rose above me, entering me in a single thrust as my sex began to tighten around him. He remained motionless, filling me to the brim and allowing me to adjust to his size. However, I couldn't remain still. Instead, I pressed against him, feeling his balls smack my butt.

Michael leaned down and took one of my nipples into his mouth while I continued to writhe beneath him. He pulled all the way out and slowly entered me again. Torturing me. He withdrew and slammed back in. I came apart in a hot rush of liquid around his cock.

"Lily! Jesus Christ." Michael froze.

I felt his cock jerk as he came inside me, triggering a second climax from deep within.

It felt as though I had been shuddering under him for ages, but it was probably only a couple of minutes. I kept my legs and arms wrapped around him as he collapsed on top of me and rolled onto his side.

MICHAEL

"I'VE COME TO THE CONCLUSION THAT YOU'RE GOING to kill me one of these days."

"You'd die happy," Lily whispered, snuggling into my side.

I cradled her against my body. Our legs were intertwined, and her arm caressed my back, touching my hip and ass gently. Then she squeezed my cheek, causing me to grow hard against her hip.

"Lily, rest."

I tucked her wandering hand under my arm, then started to smooth my hand over her belly. She turned and lay on her back as I moved further down the bed and placed kisses all over her abdomen.

"Michael?"

I met her eyes. My own were filled with questions.

"Will you still love me when I'm big and round like a dumpling?"

I laughed. But then I realized she was serious, and it looked like she had tears in her eyes.

I quickly moved up Lily's body and rested my elbows on either side of her, keeping my weight off her belly. "I love you with every breath I take. You and this baby—these babies—are my whole world. I already love your changing shape." I grinned and leaned down to kiss her nipples. "Do you think you'll get to keep these boobs?"

I laughed when she swatted me on the shoulder. "Lily, I promise you that no matter how much weight you put on, whether through pregnancy or not, I will always love you. I love what's in here the most," I told her, placing a hand over her heart.

"You've made me cry," Lily said through her tears.

God, she nearly had me in tears. I leaned forward and kissed her tears away.

"I'm looking forward to being a mom to our babies. But what about when I'm so big I can't see my toes?" She wailed.

Was she serious? "Lily, please listen to me. I love

you and always will. Besides, when you have a big belly, you'll just have to lie there and let me do whatever I want." I grinned.

"Now you're being evil," she sniffled into a tissue.

"It's our wedding night. All I'm doing is trying to stop you from crying. It hurts when I see tears in your eyes."

"I'm sorry. I just get a bit panicky every now and then when I remember we're having twins."

"Oh, babe." I brushed the hair back from her face and placed kisses on her eyes, nose, and finally, her mouth. "I tried not to think about that too much tonight, but yeah, it's scary. But we have a big family who will be there every step of the way." I smiled to reassure her. "Anyway, remember Lucien said he wanted one."

My comment had the desired effect.

Lily chuckled. "Talking about Lucien. I'm going to try to set up a date with him and my friend Sabrina when she gets back to the States.

That's not a good idea.

"Ah, Lily. I'm not sure that will go as well as you'd like. Lucien is stubborn, and he hates setups. It might be best to leave it be for now and see how they interact when we're all together."

I pulled her closer, not leaving an inch between us. I enjoyed lying in bed with the woman I loved in my arms, just talking. Oh, yeah, I loved the sex, but there was something to be said for just talking. Even though my dick was hard as fuck.

Her hand grasped my dick. She ran her thumb over the tip and lowered her lips to my chest.

"Lily," I growled. "We're going to sleep now. We need to recharge our batteries for the morning."

"I'll rest after I've sucked you off," she said, biting one of my nipples. She straddled me as I reached for her hips.

I arched into her, knowing it wouldn't take long with her mouth wrapped around me. My breathing became heavy as she started kissing and licking her way down my body. She swirled her tongue in my navel while her pebbled nipples rubbed my groin.

I held my breath as she reached the tip. Of course, she avoided the area where I wanted her the most. Lily kissed my hips and moved down my legs, tickling my feet.

Grinning, she slowly moved up between my legs while removing the pins from her hair and tossing them aside. At some point, she had removed the garter and placed it on her wrist, making me wonder what she had planned. With all the erotic books she read, she was always coming up with new things to try. I was just surprised that neither one of us had ended up in the hospital.

Lily opened my legs, leaned down between them, and licked me from my perineum to my balls, which she took into her mouth.

My stomach was already wet from leaking in excitement as she started working her way up to the crown. She swirled her tongue around while holding my gaze. She quickly sucked the tip into her mouth. Fuck, I nearly blew.

Having a naked goddess on top of me was driving me crazy.

Lily released me, then, with a wicked grin, she removed her garter and slipped it onto my cock, keeping it near the head. She started to tighten it, winding it around my dick as she would a band in her hair. The pressure was unbearable. When she couldn't tighten it anymore, she used her hands to roll it down to the base. A fucking cock ring! She had improvised and made a cock ring!

I couldn't breathe. I couldn't think. Fireworks shot through my body, and my cock leaked uncontrollably, desperate to ejaculate. She bent her head, licked up all the precum, and moved on to the ring.

I just hoped I wouldn't shoot all over my stomach before she wrapped her hot little mouth around me. "Argh... Fuck... Lily," I panted.

"I could kick myself. I forgot to bring a scarf for your balls."

I shut my eyes, trying to catch my breath, so I wouldn't come from her words. What she was doing and saying was pure torture, which the little minx knew damn well.

"Lily...please."

She squeezed my balls with her hands and moved upwards along my cock. She dipped her head, licking the throbbing vein along my cock, and sucked as much of me as she could into her mouth. Working her way back up to the tip, she dragged the garter off and tossed it over her shoulder.

With one powerful suck, I was in her mouth, touching the back of her throat, as she hummed and swallowed around me.

"Ahhh," I roared in release. Lily let me slip from her mouth, but I couldn't stop shuddering. It went on and on. I breathed heavily and wondered how I managed to climax so intensely again. I knew it was all thanks to Lily. "Fucking hell, woman! Get your body up here. I don't think I can move."

She smirked. "Good, huh? Let me grab a cloth to clean your stomach."

With that, Lily climbed out of bed and walked naked toward the bathroom.

LILY

I woke up to find Michael lying on his side with his head in his hand, watching as his other hand caressed my belly. His face darkened with a serious expression as he watched me. I reached out and caressed his jaw, bringing his attention up to my face. He had tears in his eyes.

My heart fluttered with worry. "Michael, what is it?"

He leaned forward and placed small kisses where our babies nestled. "Twins. We're having twins, Lily. Until you came along, I never thought I'd father a child. In about six months, I'll be a father of two." His voice broke as he rose up and kissed my lips. "Thank you."

I started to cry when I heard Michael say thank you. Instead of reaching for a tissue, I grabbed his head and pulled him close. "I'd be lost without you," I whispered, leaning in to kiss him.

I wrapped one leg around his hip and used my heel to pull him closer, wanting him to ease the ache that had been building since I'd awoken from an erotic dream involving Michael and his Harley. At least my dream hadn't ended as wetly as Michael's had.

Michael brought me back to the present when he started to pull away. "I need to get the door."

"What?" I asked, resting back on my elbows.

"I ordered breakfast."

Then, there was a knock on the door, which I had obviously missed the first time.

"One minute," he shouted to whoever was delivering the breakfast.

Watching Michael jump up from the bed in all his naked glory was painful. His cock jutted forward, and his balls hung heavily below. He grabbed some sweatpants from the top of his bag, turned back toward me, and shoved his legs into them. Yes, I licked my lips. It was impossible not to.

He noticed my "get back in bed" look. Placing his

hands on his hips, he stood in front of me, grinning, while I watched his cock twitch.

"Um, are you sure you can answer the door?" I smirked, but took pity on him. I climbed out of bed and grabbed a robe from the closet. There was no way he could answer the door in his current state.

With slightly unsteady legs, I gave him a gentle pat as I walked past. Swaying my butt slightly, I continued toward the door, hearing Michael groan. I refused to turn around in case I caught him stroking himself.

My breathing was slightly uneven with lust as I opened the door for the waiter to bring the tray of food inside. As he walked past me, I caught the scent of hot maple syrup. Nothing is as delicious as pancakes dripping with syrup, my all-time favorite breakfast.

While the waiter set the table, I walked to the floor-to-ceiling windows and looked out at the mountains. I loved living close to so much natural beauty, especially in the winter when it snowed. I loved sports that took place in the snow. I'd been told that I wore my first pair of skis when I was three. Of course, I couldn't remember that far back, but I'd seen photographs and heard my parents talk about it numerous times before they died.

I would have to give the snow a miss that coming winter because I'd be close to delivering, unless I went into labor early.

"Lily, come and sit." Michael took hold of my elbow and led me toward the table. "Where did you go?" he asked, smiling.

He had already placed pancakes and syrup on my plate, not to mention steaming decaf coffee in a cup to the side.

My stomach growled as I cut a piece of pancake with a fork. "I was thinking about missing the snow this coming season." I smiled. "Not that I'm complaining." I smoothed a hand over my belly.

"I'll take you out in the snow at my parents' place. But don't get your hopes up. We'll stay close to the house and use one of the gentler horses to pull the sleigh."

I must have been glowing with happiness because I jumped up from my seat, wrapped my arms around Michael's neck, and planted a kiss on his lips. "I can't wait. And when our babies are old enough, we can teach them to ski."

Michael started to scowl. "I think we should wait

until they're at least twenty before we put skis on them."

I pulled back slightly and looked into his eyes, trying to figure out if he was joking, but he looked serious. "Michael, you're being ridiculous," I told him, taking my seat again.

"My daughters should spend their time reading or playing with dolls."

Barely holding back my laughter, I replied, "Our sons will love skiing and playing rugby with their father and uncles." I couldn't hold it in anymore and started to laugh.

"Mmm," Michael mumbled, then started to attack his plate of everything under the sun. "It could be one of each. A little girl who looks just like her mama." He paused. "Hmmm, I like that idea. She still isn't putting on skis."

I rolled my eyes as I continued to munch on the pancakes. Michael was being ridiculous. I watched him shove fork after fork of food into his mouth before he finally paused to drink his coffee.

"What?"

"You do realize you're being an idiot."

He gave me a wicked grin, set his coffee cup back

on the table, stood up, and walked around the table with determination in his eyes.

He slowly sauntered around the table, turned my chair toward him, gave me a quick kiss, and picked me up into his arms. "We haven't made love this morning, which I'm going to correct right now." On his way into the bedroom, he grabbed the syrup from the table.

EPILOGUE
MICHAEL

LILY SAT NEXT TO ME ON THE MCKENZIE HOLDING private plane while I thought about my wife. Hours earlier, she had been naked, having syrup licked and sucked off her body. We had made a huge mess, but it had all been worth it. I would have been ready for round two if Ruben hadn't knocked on the door. He took us to the private airport where the jet was housed.

Our destination was Molokai in the Hawaiian Islands. It was where Lily's parents had spent their honeymoon. It meant a lot to Lily, and it meant a lot to me, too.

I saw emotion wash over her face as the jet dropped softly from the crystal-blue sky to the lush green ground below. The anticipation of what awaited us on the island was intense, and I couldn't wait to see the delight on Lily's face when we arrived.

The End
Playing with Fire is Sebastian's story.

DEAR READER

Thank you for reading *A McKenzie Wedding,* and thank you for your reviews! It's really appreciated.

Subscribe with your email to be alerted about new releases, sales, and events.

http://lexibuchanan.net

OTHER BOOKS BY AUTHOR

Hawke's Ridge

Maddox · Colton (2026)

Den Hollows

One of Six · Two of Six (2026)

Den of Filth (New MC Series 2025)

Reckless Wilder (2026)

Fifth Realm Series (Romantasy)

Quiver of Chaos · Wings & Arrows (2026)

Standalone Romantasy

Persephone Unchained

Tallulah James Mystery

*Dead and a Murder or Two · Dead and the Wedding Crashers ·
Dead and a Deadly Deed · Dead and a Best Friend*

Boston Bay Vikings

*Camden · Bennett · Ethan · Sutton · Carter · Bryson · Ivan · Theo
· Noah · Knox · Jericho · Roman*

Boston Bay Vikings Minor League

Lake · Rhodes · Nikoli · Dario · Madden · Bradford

Single Titles

Butterflies and Darkness · Come Back to Me · Indecent Villain · Lawful · Love Stryker · Tears in the Rain · Whispers of Yesterday

Holiday Season

Holiday Kisses in the Snow · Jingle Bells

Romantic Suspense Series

Twenty Eight Days · The Next Victim (2025)

Blossom Creek

Christmas at Emelia's · A Rake in Blossom Creek · Heatwave in Blossom Creek · Secret Love in Blossom Creek · Mischief in Blossom Creek · Runaway Bride in Blossom Creek · Naughty & Nice in Blossom Creek

Bad Boy Rockers

My Brother's Girl · Past Sins · My Best Friend's Sister · Never Let Go · Saving Jace · Silent Night (Novella)

Kincaid Sisters

Meant to be Mine · You Were Always Mine · Will You be Mine

McKenzie Brothers

Playing with the Boss · A McKenzie Wedding (Novella) · Playing with Fire · Playing with Desire · Playing with Trouble · Playing with their Hearts · A McKenzie Christmas (Novella)

De La Fuente Family (McKenzie Spinoff)

Love in Montana · Love in Purgatory · Love in Bloom · Love in Country · Love in Flame · Love in Game · Love in Education

McKenzie Cousins

INDECENT VILLAIN
A DARK MAFIA ROMANCE

My parents descended into the ground while I stood
motionless and unresponsive to the penetrating
darkness that was Tiberius Beckett.

He moved into my home and I realized that the man
had two sides, and he showed me his true face. I liked
him. He became my obsession, as I became his.
Together, we did some bad things.

Do you want to know more about Tiberius Beckett?
Then let me tell you about my indecent villain.

Available Now!

INDECENT VILLAIN SNEAK PEAK

Prologue

Kinsley

Fragile.

I feel like I'm going to fracture into a thousand pieces.

I stand silent and motionless beside my parents' graves, rain soaking me to the skin. The wind whistles around my body as I remain unresponsive to the penetrating darkness directed at me by Tiberius Beckett, my father's brother. The man stands tall in his dark suit, his piercing gaze seeming to search for something within me, as if he knows a secret I'm not even aware of. Despite the storm raging around us, his presence feels more unsettling than the howling wind.

My tears mix with the rain and flow down my cold cheeks. The priest speaks loudly and clearly, but his words blend as my mind refuses to comprehend them. I swallow hard as my mother's casket is lowered into the earth. Then that of my father follows. It is the end for them, and for me, too. Tiberius, at my father's request, has become my legal guardian. He doesn't want me, just as I do not want him. I tell myself I'll endure for the next two weeks until I turn eighteen. It's not long, but it feels like an eternity.

I pray that I survive the man with silver eyes.

But no one survives Tiberius Beckett.

Tiberius

Fragile.

Kinsley looks like the wind will blow her over any second. The girl does not trust me. She will. My fingers yearn to stretch across the space between us and take her in my arms. I am a hard man. But with Kinsley, my heart is fucking mush. She is my vulnerability. The girl has been in my head for a while now. It kills me to stand here and watch her suffer alone.

She is unaware of the danger she is in, just as she is unaware that my men are hidden around the cemetery to keep her safe. Me too. However, they know she is their priority. I can take care of myself, but

Kinsley cannot. She needs me, even if she doesn't realize it yet.

The rain falls harder as my brother and his wife are now in the ground. Other mourners and the priest take their leave, while Kinsley and I remain. I stare at her. Kinsley lifts her face, her eyes finding mine. I don't look away, and neither does she. We stand there in silence as the rain soaks us both. In that moment, I know that I will do whatever it takes to keep the defiant young woman safe, even if it means revealing my true feelings.

Chapter One

Three days after the funeral, the rain continues to fall. The gardens have turned into fields of mud, and even the long driveway has puddles. My grand home looks gothic surrounded by the dark clouds and rain, but in the sun, it is beautiful. I've always found the house to be too spacious for our small family. The house once bustled with numerous servants, but that was before my time and before my father's as well. Grandfather used to tell me about the garden parties his mother hosted when he was six. Sadly, not long after that, there was a war. He said most of the servants left and took up arms for their country—mostly the men, but some of the women did too, I guess.

Sighing, I consider my predicament. Tiberius is a strange man and has the power to unnerve me. I think back to my younger years but can't really put my finger on when I started to feel that way. Maybe it had more to do with my father being unsettled around his brother than anything else. I must have picked up on his unease and let it affect me. However, Tiberius does nothing to help dispel those feelings around him. I think he enjoys it. I'm not like my father, though. I won't let the man push me around. I may have been showing weakness since my parents died, but no more. I'm not a little moth who needs nurturing. I'm nearly eighteen years old but feel older.

If I'm honest with myself, there is a slither of happiness within me that I will no longer be held prisoner in my home. My parents were afraid of something in the months leading to their deaths and had kept me home with a private tutor. I don't miss the city, but I do miss going into town, even if it is only for a cup of coffee while I watch the world go by. It's better than being locked up inside the Lake House.

I press a hand to my stomach, trying to quell the bundle of nerves that suddenly rises as I watch a large black car appear through the trees along the driveway. The wheels kick up muddy water as Tiberius brings the beast to a stop close to the front entrance. Another car, this one silver and sleek, pulls in beside the black one. The man has arrived, along with my parents' attorney.

Tiberius climbs from the driver's side of the car, while another man emerges from the passenger seat. They exchange words.

The attorney, Mr. Arnold Fielding, exits his car and runs for the front door. Tiberius takes one step and seems to be frozen to the spot. His head suddenly turns, and his gray eyes lift and find mine. Stunned, I gasp, but I refuse to look away first. My heart thumps heavily behind my breastbone. How did he know I was watching, and from where? He snaps his attention back to his passenger, a man in jeans and a tee. Unnerved, I head into the bathroom and splash cold water onto my face. I pat it dry with a fluffy towel. The mirror before me reflects my drawn expression. Dark circles are prominent beneath my eyes, the color matching my long hair.

A knock on my bedroom door draws my attention. I swallow hard, knowing there will be no escaping the next hour or so. Today is the reading of the will, followed by lunch with Tiberius. I am overjoyed.

Another knock.

"One moment," I shout.

I slide my feet into the shoes I kicked off earlier and take one last glance in the mirror. The dark color of my midi dress does nothing for my washed-out look. I open the door and catch the impatient look on the housekeeper's face.

"About time," Martha snaps before briskly turning away.

I roll my eyes and inhale, holding my breath for a few seconds before slowly exhaling. It helps center me when I know I am about to face danger. That is what Tiberius Beckett is to me—the devil himself.

And there he is.

His dark-gray eyes follow me as I move down the staircase, his body remaining still like a predator. I refuse to let him see the nerves that threaten to break me in his presence. He is the kind of man who, if you give him an inch, he will take a mile.

I come to a stop at the end of the stairs and hesitate. My father's office will be used for the reading of stand my father. I have only ever seen you from a distance, but now I am your ward. Why?"

Tiberius frowns when his eyes land on me. "None of that matters now."

I force my gaze to the lawyer. "If Tiberius thought he was getting the house, then am I correct to assume my father made a previous will? What was in it?"

"That doesn't—"

"Tell her," Tiberius snaps.

Mr. Fielding takes a sip of the glass of water in front of him, and says, "In your father's previous will, he left the house to Tiberius Beckett and explained why. As Tiberius said, the eldest male descendant was to inherit the house."

"My father was Jude Elliott. How are you a Beckett?"

"That piece of paper in your hand will not stand up in court when I have my lawyer file an objection." The man totally ignores me and speaks to Mr. Fielding.

A headache brews behind my temples, and I want to leave the room. I feel sorry for Mr. Fielding, who has done nothing but read my parents' wishes. Tiberius reminds me of a bull ready to charge. His nostrils flare, and his large body tightens with suppressed anger. He is a tall man who obviously takes good care of himself. The muscle he possesses is unable to hide behind the clothes he wears.

I sense the tension in the room escalating as Tiberius's anger becomes palpable. I need to diffuse the situation before it escalates further. My hands feel sweaty and my mouth is dry, but I have to say something to calm Tiberius down.

"I don't want the house. He can have it." I rush the words out and bring the two men to silence. In truth, the house is the only home I've ever known, but I always planned to leave when I turned eighteen.

"What?" Tiberius shakes his head. "What did you say?"

I swallow hard, and say, "You can have the house." I turn my gaze to Mr. Fielding. "You can arrange that, right?"

"Actually"—the older man sighs—"nothing can be done until you turn twenty-one."

Tiberius releases a string of curse words, some of which raise my eyebrows in shock. As difficult as it is to ignore his strong presence, I turn away from him and give my full attention to Mr. Fielding. I need to concentrate.

"I'm assuming there is a clause about selling the house."

"It states that you must live in the house until you turn twenty-one, after which time, you can leave and pass on ownership. However, your father stipulated that ownership could only be passed to Tiberius Beckett."

"Let me get this straight. My father left me the house, yes?" He nods. "But I have to continue living here until I turn twenty-one, at which point he expects me to hand the house over to him." I point toward the beast of a man.

"That is correct."

"Why didn't he just leave the house to him in the first place? This doesn't make any sense." I get my unsteady legs under me and stand. "What about college? How will I go if I must live here?"

"That detail we will discuss at another time," Tiberius says, calm once more. He takes out a piece of gum and moves it between his fingers. Is he trying to quit smoking?

"My father was afraid of you." It takes courage, but I manage to hold his gaze. "Why would he make me your ward?"

"I'm the only one who would have you."

"That's not quite—"

"Mr. Fielding," snaps Tiberius. "Thank you for your time this morning. I will bring my niece into your office next week to sign the documents you have for her." He ushers the lawyer from the room.

My refusal to join Tiberius for lunch has garnered his anger once more. The man takes my arm and drags me into the formal dining room, where he pushes me into a chair beside the one at the head of the table, which he takes.

"You need to eat." His large hands tighten around his cutlery. "You've lost weight since the last time I saw you."

In truth, I am hungry. The food in front of me looks more appetizing than anything Martha has prepared since my parents died.

"Hmm," I mutter as I straighten in the chair and start to eat. Tiberius watches me with a calculated look on his face as he continues eating.

The food is pleasant, which puts me at ease and leads me to ask, "Will you be moving in?"

He nods.

"Good. At least we'll get something edible."

He pauses with a fork of beef near his lips. "Explain that comment." He places his knife and fork on the plate and sits back, his gaze unwavering.

"Since my parents died, the food hasn't been good." I sigh. "I'm not allowed in the kitchen to make my own, so it's no wonder that I've lost weight. I hate tuna, which Martha serves me on crackers for lunch daily."

"I shudder at the thought," he says. In his next breath, he shouts, "Martha!"

The woman who hates me comes dashing into the room. "Sir?"

My cheeks flush hotly, and I silently plead that he won't drop me in it with her. Tiberius narrows his eyes on my face, and his jaw twitches.

"I will be moving into the house later today, and I expect breakfast and dinner served in this room with my niece daily, unless otherwise stated. There will be no tuna and crackers." He pauses for a moment, holding her full attention. "There will also be no seafood put on the table. Ever."

Martha shoots me a look of hatred before she says, "Yes, sir."

"My niece is the owner of this house, which means she is your employer. If you value your position here, I suggest you treat her with respect. She needs to eat, not starve. Do I make myself clear?"

"Yes."

"Yes, what?"

"Yes, sir."

Tiberius snorts. "Go." He turns to me. "I have no clue what I am supposed to do with you."

"You could ignore me, and I will ignore you."

He grins, which surprises me. He has to be the most handsome man I've ever seen. "You're too pretty to be ignored, and I'm too big and loud." He frowns. "Others will be moving into the house with me. You need to stay out of their way." He points his fork in my direction. "They are dangerous men. I will only give you this warning once. You understand me?"

It's a good thing I've eaten all my food, as my appetite suddenly disappears. "I understand." My mind whirls, wondering who they are and why he has dangerous men living with him. My outlook is certainly looking better. Maybe I won't be bored anymore. Tiberius is a large man with an equally large personality.

As my eyes rove over his features, I realize I don't

consider him my uncle. How could I when I've never known him? My curiosity about him is piqued, and while he seems slightly more approachable than he has been in the past, I decide to ask my questions.

"Are you married?"

His gray eyes shoot to mine. "No." He smirks. "Are you?"

"Considering I'm seventeen, I would have thought the answer to that question was obvious."

"If you ask me personal questions, then expect the same in return." He grins, mirth dancing in his gaze. "What else do you want to know?"

"Why have we never actually met until now?" I sit back in the chair and try to appear relaxed. I certainly feel better than I did before. Maybe I just needed something proper to eat, or what I do not want to admit, company. I'm not sure how I feel about Tiberius. That's a lie. The man with silver eyes causes parts of my body to come alive. Butterflies flutter in my belly. Maybe it's the way he looks at me. I have his sole attention, and I want to keep it.

"There are things that your mother chose to keep from you. I need some time to decide whether or not I tell you what they are."

I watch him, my curiosity stronger than ever. "Would those things change anything?"

He sits forward with his hands on the table. He intertwines his fingers. "The secret Anna and Jude kept would change everything," he says in a deep voice, his eyes blazing. "One day, I may tell you."

I frown. If I'm not mistaken, I catch something within his gaze, as though he is scared to speak of it. I'm more determined than ever to discover what my parents kept from me.

"Not today?"

"Maybe not ever." He stands and tosses his napkin on his plate. "If I do tell you, just remember they are the ones who kept you in the dark." With that, he moves toward the large doorway. He pauses with his hand on the knob and glances over his shoulder. "I will be here from this evening."

"You!" Martha hisses the moment the large front door closes behind Tiberius.

To my horror, my legs tremble at the confrontation I know is seconds away. Martha has always been an evil woman. As soon as Tiberius spoke to her, I knew she would be on me the moment he left. And here she is.

"How dare you complain, you ungrateful little bitch!" Martha charges forward, and I stumble into the wall behind me. She follows and slaps me hard across the face.

Tears fill my eyes as I cradle my throbbing cheek, too stunned to react.

"You think it matters to me that you own this house?" she scoffs. "You know nothing." Her eyes glow with unleashed anger. "I would be careful of who I become friends with, Kinsley," she sneers. "Beckett is—"

I watch her closely as her mouth pulls tight. My heart pounds in my chest while I wonder how to break free of her hold. Martha has never laid a hand on me before, but now the woman before me is finally showing her true colors. I pull myself up to my full five-foot-five height and glare at the woman.

"Do not touch me again," I say, clear and precise. "Next time, I will fight back."

Her eyes narrow. "You are brave all of a sudden." She scowls and looks out of the window. "I may not like you, but if the rumors about Tiberius are true, then I fear for you." Her arm shoots out and holds me against the wall. She is stronger than she appears. "No more whispering into that man's ear about me, or you will be very sorry." With one last shove, she turns and leaves.

I gasp and give into the tears that have been threatening to fall throughout the whole confrontation. My cheek stings as I place it against the cold window and watch the dark clouds roll over the grounds. My stomach is in turmoil. I don't understand what is going on. The one fact that I do know is that I am the ward of Tiberius Beckett. Why him? I have no idea why my father did that. Although I do not trust Martha, her words have me concerned. What does she know about the man to fear for me?

Something else has become apparent. My father knew he was going to die. The changes to his will were completed three weeks before his death. The weight of my new responsibilities as Tiberius's ward settles heavily on my shoulders as I consider the implications of my father's foresight. The realization scares me.

Scared and out of my depth, I turn away from the window. The grandeur of the dining room now seems suffocating, a stark reminder of the impending gloom that arises within me. The portrait of my father hanging on the wall seems to mock me with his knowing gaze, as if he has left behind secrets that I am now forced to uncover. The feeling of unease grows stronger, making me question everything I thought I knew about my family.

Somehow, I manage to pull myself together. I will not let Martha see how much her sharp words and slap across my face have affected me. The woman will not be working at the house for much longer if I have my way. Maybe Tiberius has his own staff that he can bring here. Anyone would be better than the bitter Martha Green.

Chapter Two

I tear off my suit and change into jeans and a tee. After fastening my biker boots, I release a frustrated growl. I don't know what the fuck to do about sweet, innocent Kinsley.

I glare out of my bedroom window, my gaze settling on the house across the lake. I open the door and step out onto the balcony. It's sparsely furnished, with just a table and two chairs, plus a comfortable chaise lounge chair. I've spent many summer nights asleep on it. The outdoors has always called to me, just like the Lake House has.

Memories always swamped me whenever I dropped in on Jude and his family. In recent years, my brother had become uneasy about those visits, which made me wonder what he might have been hiding.

As I rest on the balustrade and gaze out once more across the lake at the house, I wonder what Kinsley is up to. It's something I've wondered for a while now whenever my eyes caught on the house. Thoughts I should never have, even now. At first, it was innocent curiosity about the girl I knew my brother hadn't fathered. But over the past couple of years, I found myself unable to stay away. I've never been intro-duced to the girl until now. I made sure I always stopped by when I knew she wouldn't be home.

Kinsley grew up rather quickly and became a stunner. I shouldn't be obsessed with her. It's wrong. I know that what I'm feeling would be considered acceptable in the real world, if it weren't for the age difference. I'm not really her uncle. Never have been. Never will be. She doesn't know that yet.

One look at me covered in tattoos would disgust her. My brother never liked ink. Neither had my mother, which is why I have so many.

Kinsley doesn't remember, but when she was told about her parents' deaths, I showed up at the house. She was in shock, so I took charge of her. I held her while she stared into space. I held her some more when her tears finally came. I held her while she slept.

I should have stayed with her so she wasn't alone, but I was dealing with my own grief. Not only that, but I also had to deal with the cops and make arrangements for Jude and Anna. I took my grief and anger and went after the crew who had forced my brother's car off the road. His brakes had been cut, and as the crew chased after them, Jude wasn't able to slow down on the sharp bends of Snake Pass.

I saw the bodies and wish I hadn't. The only bit of luck that evening was that the car hadn't burst into flames.

One crew member was still at large. That was my fault. I lost it with the three my men and I had found. The last one died before he could give me a name. However, I did get one name from the other two. Cannon Edge.

That bastard would pay one day.

I turn my head at the sound of booted feet moving down the hallway outside my bedroom.

"Boss," Salem shouts, knocking on the door. "You in here?"

"Outside," I yell.

He strides out and comes to rest beside me, his gaze following mine. "Do you know what you're doing?"

"I don't have a fucking clue."

He snorts. "I haven't seen you this fucked up before."

I glare at my friend. "I'm not fucked up." My eyes stray back to the Lake House. "Edge is going to come for Kinsley."

"He won't get her. Between you, me, and Jock, we've handpicked all the men who will be around the house. She will be safe."

"Tell the men they don't touch her. Make sure they know she's my family and I will personally kill anyone who causes her harm."

"Yes, boss," Salem drawls, mirth in his voice, which I ignore.

"Prick!"

"Edgar has the weasel in the basement. You wanted to talk to him."

"I want to do more than fucking talk," I snarl.

"Who is he?" I ask Edgar.

The man tied to the chair, with blood and sweat running down his face, is not familiar to me.

"Brinkley," Edgar growls. "I overheard him bragging about knowing where Jubal is hiding out. Why the fuck he'd do that is anyone's guess."

I narrow my gaze and clench my fists. "He's either stupid for flapping his jaws or doesn't know shit, which also makes him stupid."

The man spits blood on the floor. "Fuck you! I know who you are, and you and that bitch will be next."

Before the asshole can blink, I slam my fist into his face. The chair wobbles and then crashes backward.

"Where the fuck is he?"

Although the man laughs, fear sets in. I see it in his eyes and the piss stain on his jeans.

"I lied." He laughs. "I fucking lied. I don't even know who Jubal is."

I crouch beside him as I wipe my hands on a cloth. "You see, I don't believe you. With both mine and

Edge's men looking for Jubal, it would be fucking idiotic to lie about knowing him." I glare at the piece of shit and force myself to stand. To Edgar, I say, "Find out what you can. Then turn him over to Edge."

"No way." Brinkley tugs against his bindings, struggling to break free. "He'll kill me."

Edgar laughs. "Beckett didn't say you have to be alive when I turn you over to Edge."

Pure fear erupts on Brinkley's face.

I walk away. Salem, who had kept to the background, says, "Something doesn't add up with that asshole."

That is what I've been thinking since Edgar brought him in.

Five minutes later, my phone beeps with a message from Edgar. I read it twice before sharing the info with Salem. "Edgar sent the location Brinkley gave him to Prez to get the murdering asshole."

"Fucking hell! Brinkley really was an idiot."

I trust Prez to find Jubal now. All I must do is wait. Something I've been doing since Jude died.

"Make sure the bikes are loaded on to the truck. I don't want to be traveling back and forth between the houses for now."

"They've already been loaded. When do you want to leave?"

"Now."

Salem heads off to round the men up while I stand outside in the fresh air. In truth, I don't want Kinsley in this world of mine, but whether I do or not, it doesn't matter anymore.

Kinsley's life is now tied to mine whether she likes it or not.

Chaptaer Three

I watch as four large black SUVs come up the driveway. My heart thuds in my chest with a mixture of fear and excitement. Tiberius said he would be back.

The moment he steps onto the gravel driveway, his head lifts, and those dark-gray eyes of his land on me. I don't move, and neither does he, until another man says something to him. I shake myself, questioning how the man can ensnare me so easily.

Men in jeans and tees climb from the vehicles. Out of the nine men I count, two are wearing dark suits. Tiberius has changed out of his suit into black jeans and a white tee with sunglasses perched atop his head. It's certainly a different view of the man than the one I previously had. Who are the men with him? They all look dangerous and unapproachable. Surely, they're not all moving into the house.

My head turns as I hear booted feet enter the house. Tiberius gives instructions in a loud voice, and then the footsteps start upstairs. My bedroom door is locked, but that won't keep anyone out who is determined to get inside.

A moment later, there is a knock on my door. "Ms. Kinsley, your, um, uncle, would like you to come downstairs."

I frown at the door. The voice is hesitant, which is not what I expected. Suddenly, more curious than scared, I dash to the door and pull it open. My eyes shoot wide at the huge man standing before me in a lovely dark-gray suit. He is most certainly not what I expected after the voice I heard through the door.

He smirks. "Call me Jock," he says in a calm voice. "You must be Kinsley." He holds out his hand and smiles, but then his eyes narrow as he zeroes in on the side of my face that is red and bruised. "Who did that to you?" His voice deepens.

"The girl is accident prone," Martha says, appearing out of the blue.

The large man stares into my eyes, and I silently

beg him not to say anything because I know that he knows who is responsible. He turns to the woman. "Martha, isn't it? You are wanted in the kitchen." When she hovers, he adds, "Now, woman!"

I wince, which Jock notices. "She won't touch you again. Come. He's waiting for you." I nod, trying to hide my nerves as I follow Jock down the dimly lit hallway. "Don't worry too much about the men in the house. They will leave you alone."

I hesitate at the top of the stairs. "Maybe I should have changed first."

"Nonsense. You look fine." Jock smiles. My eyes travel down my white tee to where my black jeans cling to my skin. Thick socks cover my feet. I didn't bother with my biker boots today.

"Stop fidgeting," Jock says as he shoves me into my father's office—what was my father's office. The heavy door closes behind me. If I didn't know that Tiberius was already in the room, his scent would have given him away.

"You look scared," he comments.

I turn around. "It's unnerving having strange men wandering around my home."

His eyes narrow, and then he is suddenly in front of me. A large, tattooed hand holds my jaw as he turns my face to get a better look at the bruise forming there. I doubt Martha intended on leaving such a sign that she'd hit me.

Tiberius looks into my eyes. "This is because I called her out at lunch." His jaw tightens. "I'll get rid of her."

"No!" I grab hold of his wrist before I snatch my hand back. A sizzle of electricity shoots up my arm. I swallow hard. "I mean." I sigh. "I don't know what I mean."

His fingers gently smooth over the soreness of my cheek before he steps back. "That woman—"

"Boss," a dark-skinned man interrupts us. He grins when he sees me, and I don't think I've ever seen anyone with such perfect, white teeth before.

My lips twist into a smile when I realize the man is really being friendly. "Hello," I offer.

Tiberius narrows his eyes between the two of us and snaps, "Saul! I do not pay you to drool over my"—he clears his throat—"niece."

"No, sir!" Saul snaps his focus to Tiberius, who hasn't stopped glaring. "I came to tell you the truck is five minutes out."

"Okay. Get them moving once they arrive."

Saul nods and exits the room without another glance my way.

"Are the men moving in as well?" I ask the silently brooding man. I try to ignore the fact we're dressed similarly. Thank God I left my boots off; otherwise, we'd be identical.

"Yes." He enters my space, and it takes all my will power not to back down. "You will not encourage them."

It takes me a moment to understand what he is saying. When I do, my eyes widen in surprise. "He's far too old for me." I don't add that my taste in men centers on the man in front of me.

"So dramatic." He steps back and looks irritated. "Regardless, do not speak to my men."

The sound of a loud vehicle approaching breaks the silence as the wheels crunch on the driveway.

I look out the window and frown at the eighteen-wheeler. "What is in there?"

"Furniture, among other things." He pauses in the doorway. "Do you want any of the furniture from your parents' bedroom before I have it destroyed?"

"No, thank you." That is something I do not want. "However, if you wish to get rid of my father's desk, I would like that."

He nods. "Dinner will be in an hour or so."

"Why don't you step away from the window?" Jock suggests.

"I'm curious. I've seen Tiberius every now and again over the years; however, I never actually met him until the reading of the will. I mean, he was at the funeral, but we didn't speak. My father thought he was doing the right thing by making me his ward. So, I must trust in that." It doesn't stop me from admiring the fit of his jeans and tee as he moves.

"Your father knew Beckett would protect you if he asked. You will be safe here."

I turn to Jock and frown. "You call him by his family name?"

"Habit." Jock smiles. "How about a warm drink in the kitchen. I could do with a cup of coffee myself."

"Okay." I follow beside him and come to a stop. "What are they carrying upstairs?"

"A bed."

"He doesn't want to sleep in my parents' bed, so he brought his own." I glance at Jock for confirmation.

He nods.

"I suppose that makes sense." I sigh. "There are a lot of things that do not make sense to me, though. Many in fact, and I don't know where to start."

"Let's have that cup of coffee," he suggests and leads me toward the kitchen. "Problem?" he asks when I come to a sudden stop before stepping foot inside.

"I've never been allowed inside the kitchen," I whisper.

"From what I have been told, this is your house, which means this is your kitchen." He smirks and pushes his way inside. A growl comes out of his mouth when he sees Martha at the far end of the room. "You lay a hand on this girl again, and I will show you how hard a man as big as me can hit."

Oh God.

"You took the words right out of my mouth, Jock." Tiberius moves into the room. "This is your last chance, Ms. Green." His steely eyes narrow on the woman before he shoots a look I can't decipher at Jock. "Do not bring my niece over to the dark side while I'm in the office."

"Wouldn't dream of it."

Tiberius snorts and turns his attention to me. His

eyes linger as he grabs an apple on his way out of the room.

Jock claps his hands. "Show's over. Now, can someone show us where we can make our coffee?"

"It's behind you. Nothing too fancy," a timid voice replies.

I turn to find a former employee. The young woman is maybe three years older than me. She's also the daughter of one of Martha's friends, and I'm sure she fears the vile woman too. "Thank you, Marie." I smile at her. "I didn't know you were working here again."

"Mr. Beckett called the old staff back." Marie moves closer. "I am sorry about your parents, Kinsley." She grabs my hand and squeezes.

"Thank you," I say, choking on the words.

I turn my attention to Jock, who's pouring two cups of coffee. He passes me a cup, then places a hand to my back and guides me back out along the hallway.

"The girl seemed nice," he says when we reach the living room.

"Marie is." I sit at one end of the sofa and inhale the rich aroma before I take a sip. "This is very good."

"I made it, so of course it is." He chuckles. "No one comes between me and my coffee."

"Did Tiberius ask you to be nice to me?"

His eyes dance. "He told me not to let you out of my sight."

"Hmm," I mutter.

I sit back and listen to the men putting the bed together upstairs. Hammering comes from the office, which I ignore. I don't want to know what other changes are taking place. Instead, I wonder about Jock. I sense the man was truly angry when he discovered I was hit. He will follow Tiberius's orders in the end, which means I can't trust him as much as I want to. It would be nice to not be so alone anymore.

I guess I will be safe from the outside world in the house. But will I be safe from Tiberius?

Available Now!

ONE OF SIX
A DARK ROMANCE

Six brothers

Six heartbreakers

Six Den Hollows

Essex Redd, the youngest of six brothers at the age of nineteen. My father was murdered four years ago, and we know who did it. What we don't know is why. Things get complicated when I fall in love with the killer's daughter. As the truth begins to unravel, I realize that Bea and my family are in more danger than anyone thought.

My name is Beatrice Alexandria Lincoln. I prefer to be called Bea. I live in the town of Mount Sterling, which is known for its old-fashioned charm and Southern hospitality, and residents like my parents keep those traditions alive. I long for a life of my own choosing. When my mother dies suddenly, my eyes are opened to the harsh reality of what it truly means to be a Lincoln.

My father has no idea what I will do to protect the people I love.

Available Now!

Chapter One - Beatrice

Beatrice Alexandria Lincoln. This has been my name since the day I was born eighteen years ago. My parents, Richard, and Elisabeth are patrons of the town of Mount Sterling in the Deep South. Sweet tea, served with a side of sweet fancy, is the official offering to visitors to the house.

I often wonder if anyone else would appreciate my life more than I do. My father is the one who bought and paid for my entire existence.

We live in a white mansion, a five-minute walk from the edge of town. It's where the wealth is. Lush gardens, sleek and shiny vehicles, designer flower beds, and fake people. The town of Mount Sterling is known for its old-fashioned charm and Southern hospitality, and residents like my parents keep those traditions alive. Despite the material wealth that surrounds us, I sometimes long for a simpler life. My father is the mayor. My grandfather is the judge, and my uncle is the sheriff. You see what I mean?

The residents want to be in my parents' circle of friends. They push their offspring in my direction, hoping that being my friend will bring them recognition. I don't bother anymore. I have one friend and she's enough. It can be lonely living in a community where people are more interested in your family position than who you really are as a person.

I feel like a robot. A Stepford wife. Every waking moment is planned, even more so since I graduated from high school. I want to go to college. Not that I am interested in any field, but to get away from my family. I'm not sure that is going to turn out to my advantage, as my parents are against it. If my parents hadn't been on my back all the time about grades, maybe I would have fought harder. But now it's too late.

My skin itches against the cotton fabric of the dress I wear. The humidity makes sweat run between my breasts and down my back. The weather makes me sleepy as I listen to the drone of my mother and her three closest friends. The suffocating feeling of being trapped in this picture-perfect life is over-whelming. I long for freedom, for a chance to discover who I really am beyond my family's expectations.

Today's meeting is for them to decide which of their sons I will date first. I don't want to date any of them. I have no choice. Richard Lincoln has spoken. I feel like a pawn in their game of social status and tradition, with no say in my own future. The weight of their expectations crushes me.

I smile in all the right places, only half listening. A loud vibration shakes the China on the dining room table. My eyes wander out the window as a slight smile appears on my lips. Motorcycles roar past the house. The men who ride them live across the railroad tracks in Den Hollows. There are no white mansions with manicured lawns in Den Hollows.

I want to be free like them. Free to ride like the wind through the town without a care in the world.

Seconds later, my dream shatters as the sirens announce the arrival of the sheriff's deputies. I sigh, wishing my uncle's deputies would leave the men alone.

They are real men. No tailored three-piece suits covering their pasty white—sometimes overweight— bodies. Jeans and T-shirts cover their muscular frames. I imagine it's one of them every time I use my vibrator.

A blush covers my cheeks as I turn my attention

back to my mother. I wish I'd paid more attention, because ten minutes later they agree on something I missed.

As mother walks them out, I go to my bedroom and close the door with a huge sigh of relief. I throw the clothes off and into the hamper. In the shower, I scrub my hair to get the hairspray out, which Mom insists on before I scrub my body until I'm red and clean.

When I'm done, I brush out my red hair and put on shorts and a vest. I go downstairs barefoot and follow the sound of my mother's voice into the kitchen.

She gives me a scathing look, her mouth tight. "Beatrice, I asked you to be polite. I didn't expect it to be so difficult for you."

"I was there. I served the sweet tea and the fancies. I smiled and spoke when spoken to. What did I do wrong?" I clench my fists behind my back, angry at the words I force from my lips when I want to say so much more.

"Honestly, child." She grabs my arm and drags me through the house. "My friends noticed when you were distracted by the window." Her eyes narrow. "Those Redd boys and their gang of thieves."

"They're not thieves, Mom." The second the words are out of my mouth; I feel a sharp pinch on my arm. "Ouch."

"You watch what you say to me!" she snaps. "Your father was right. You need a man to keep you in line."

"I'm eighteen. I want to go to college and get an education." I pull my arm free, feeling the bruise already marking my skin. "Dad said he would think about it."

Mom sits down. "Yes, well, your father has thought about it. You are going to get married. We can keep an eye on you here until that happens. Make sure you stay pure for your husband."

My mouth falls open.

"Oh, Beatrice, stop catching flies." Her eyes sweep over me in disgust. "You have a date with Jason Greenwood tomorrow night. You will behave like a lady or face your father. Do I make myself clear?"

"Jason? Isn't he old?"

"He's a respectable lawyer in town. He just turned thirty." Her eyes narrow. "Didn't I ask you a question?"

"Yes, Ma'am," I say. "I'm clear." Inside, where no one can hear me, I scream.

"Instead of sulking around the house, go to the store and buy some milk."

It's on the tip of my tongue to tell her to go get it herself in her nice, air-conditioned car. But I don't. My dad's hand hurts bad.

I take the ten dollars she hands me. "Get yourself something to drink so you don't faint on the way home."

As soon as I slip my feet into a pair of ballet flats, I step outside, and the heat envelops me. This summer is hot.

The houses I pass make me sick. None of the people who live in them deserve it. They don't care about anyone but making more money for themselves and kissing my family's ass.

I walk through the gates that are supposed to keep others out, wondering which guard will lose his job because the men from Den Hollows rode through. The men ask for trouble by doing what they did today. Part of me doesn't blame them. If I was told to stay away from somewhere, I'd want to go. The only difference is that I wouldn't have the courage to do it.

I walk through the pretty town, past the barber shop, the post office, and the library on the corner. I cross the street and pass a few restaurants and the sheriff's office. I turn right and walk towards the big grocery store.

The store is quiet as I enter, and I take a moment to stand under one of the air conditioning units in the ceiling. My eyes go wide when I catch my reflection in a mirror. My red hair is completely dried and sticks up everywhere. There is no rhyme or reason to it.

"Beatrice, how are you?"

"I'm fine, Mr. Gleeson. Mama sent me for milk." I sound like my ten-year-old self. "And a popsicle." I like the owner of this store. He has always looked the same—slim, with a head full of white hair, a big nose, and dark eyes that miss nothing hidden behind large black specks.

He smiles warmly, revealing a row of perfectly straight teeth. "You always liked the popsicles."

"I deserve two today. Or maybe three."

"You know where everything is." He smiles. "I'll ring you up when you're ready."

"Thank you." I move away but pause. "Mr. Gleeson?"

"Yes, Beatrice."

"Did you see Den Hollows come through town?"

Mr. Gleeson's smile falters slightly before he answers. "I'd have to be dead not to know when they ride those bikes." He winks. "The sheriff's men chased them right back out of town."

"Oh!" Disappointment settles in my stomach, and I'm not sure why. It's not like I know how to talk to them. If I did, I would feel my father's hand afterwards.

I walk over to the popsicles, pick out a pink one and bite into it with my teeth. As soon as the popsicle bursts it's wrapping, I lick it slowly, savoring the taste. I close my eyes and sigh with pleasure. I wrap my tongue around the ice before taking it into my mouth. It tastes so good.

The sound of a growl makes my eyes open wide. My heart stutters in my chest. The Redd brothers stand on the other side of the store with all eyes focused on my mouth. It has been a long time since I have seen one of them. I don't think I've ever seen them all together—Atilio, Nico, Boone, Galen, Ridge, and Essex. Six brothers. Six heartbreakers. Six Den Hollows.

Chapter Two - Essex

My eyes focus on the girl with the brightest hair I've

ever seen. I know who she is. Everyone does. Beatrice Lincoln. The mayor's daughter.

My instant response to her has nothing to do with her parentage, but the girl herself. Curves to make a guy's mouth water. Curly hair that falls in a mess around her face and down her back, over her breasts. It's more orange than red. Fiery.

What freezes me and my brothers to the floor is the way her tongue curls around the popsicle in her hand. The way she licks with her pink tongue, and then heat slides through me when her mouth wraps around the ice.

My dick is so hard that I need to pound something. Preferably into her sweet pussy.

She lifts her gaze and sees the six of us standing watching her. When her eyes land on me my dick jerks behind my zipper. I have never had such a visceral reaction to anyone before and it makes me angry.

Just my luck it's the one girl none of us can touch. Probably one of the only virgins to graduate high school.

I glance at my brothers and wonder what they're thinking. How can one innocent girl bring the six of us to a stop.

Ridiculous.

Still, no one moves.

"Gleeson," I shout. My brother to the right jumps, but I bring us back to the present and the reason we are here.

The girl grabs up two more popsicles, turns, grabs some milk and then high tails it toward the exit.

I feel like I can finally breathe.

Chapter Three - Beatrice

Mr. Gleeson runs toward me as I head for the exit. I toss him the ten dollars and head for the door. I stop. What if Mr. Gleeson needs help?

I'm not sure how long I stand in the doorway, but the next thing I know I'm being grabbed from behind. I don't even struggle when I look down and see strong hands leading to leather-clad arms around my stomach. When I inhale, the man behind me even smells wonderful. I'm tempted to turn my face to his neck and take another whiff. He'd probably think I was crazy if I buried my nose there.

"Aren't you going to fight me, little girl?" His rough voice breaks me out in goose bumps.

"Atilio," Mr. Gleeson's voice makes him turn around so we're both facing the shopkeeper. "Please put Beatrice down. She's a good girl. Not like..." he winces.

The tall man is the oldest brother, only twenty-six. He was born Atilio Junior, but when his father died four years ago, he dropped the Junior. At least that's what I heard. I may not see the Redd men, but I know all about them. I'm good at listening when others think I'm not.

"I like it in his arms." He starts to move and Mr. Gleeson winces as we pass him. "Make sure the doors are locked."

He carries me to the back of the store where his brothers are waiting. They are all handsome men with a mixture of dark and medium brown hair.

"She's checking us out," another brother says with a grin on his face and amusement dancing in his bright green eyes.

I narrow mine. "I wonder who I should kick in the balls first," I reply.

His eyes go wide, and he moves in front of me. "I can assure you that if you ever get near my balls, you will either be on your knees sucking my dick or on your back with your legs spread."

"Dipshit!" one brother slaps the younger one on the back of the head.

"Excuse Ridge, all his manners were knocked out of him years ago when Atilio dropped him on his head."

"Fuck you, Boone!"

"Guys," Mr. Gleeson appears. "Leave them alone. Atilio, put her down. Ridge, your mother needs to wash your mouth out with soap and water."

My feet hit the ground so suddenly that I lose my footing. Another brother steps forward. "I'm the nice brother. Ignore my twin. I'm Galen." He holds out his hand.

I take it quickly as he begins to pull away. "I'm Beatrice."

His face splits into a huge grin. "Your popsicles are melting."

I blink, surprised.

"Stop flirting," Atilio says. "We've got shit to do." He grabs my hips and sits me down on a freezer lid. "You, don't move."

"Okay." I look into his brown eyes and see flecks of gold. *He has kind eyes,* I think as he pulls away.

I'm curious about what's going on here. Mr. Gleeson isn't afraid of them. So, they can't be robbing the store. Atilio and his brothers are bigger than me. They are over six feet tall. They all wear jeans and a T-shirt with leather jackets of different styles.

I know who each of the brothers are, even though this is the first time I've met them, or rather, the first time I've been in the same room with them.

I absentmindedly tear into another popsicle, sucking out all the melted liquid before pushing the last piece of ice up. I tilt my head and wrap my tongue around it before sucking it into my mouth. It's a little too long to fit, but I crunch it down.

"Those damn things should be illegal in your hands," Atilio says, rearranging his crotch. My eyes fly to his as my face flushes with heat. He gently removes the last one from my hands and smiles. "My brothers won't get shit done if they're busy watching these getting sucked into that pretty mouth."

My cheeks burn. "What are you doing here?" I ask, watching them start to read the labels on the crates in the back of the store. Anything to get their attention away from me and my mouth.

"Looking for something," Boone tells me, his dark eyes fixed on my legs in the shorts I wear. I'm surprised my mom let me out of the house in this outfit. It's tight and shows my curves in a way my mom wouldn't like.

Do the Redds like the way I look? I'm sure they're as curious about me, as I am about them.

"Found it!" a voice shouts.

"Don't drop it." Nico.

The sudden banging on the windows of the store freezes their movements. Mr. Gleeson gasps. "It's the sheriff." He goes pale.

Only one thing to do. I shuffle forward. "I suppose you have a truck in the back?"

"What of it?" Essex, the youngest, hisses and takes a step toward me.

Atilio holds out a hand. "Cut it out."

"If Mr. Gleeson doesn't open the front doors, the sheriff will drive around the back."

"She's right." Boone.

"Let me go out there with Mr. Gleeson and open up. I'll think of something to distract him. Just please don't leave until his car is gone." I wince. "My father will be furious if he finds out I helped you."

"We can't trust her!" Essex argues.

"I trusted you not to hurt me. I have no quarrel with you. Let me do this." I look at Atilio.

"Don't burn us," Atilio says.

"I won't." I look at each brother in turn, remembering which face goes with which name.

Mr. Gleeson takes my hand and pulls me through the store. "Are you sure, Beatrice?"

"You've always been kind to me, Mr. Gleeson, without asking for anything in return." I stop to wave to my uncle. "I'm doing this for you and them. They don't deserve the town treating them the way they do."

"Thank you." He slides the key into the lock. "If you ever need anything, come to me, okay?" He meets my gaze briefly.

I nod as my uncle bursts into the store. "Sheriff," Mr. Gleeson stutters. He sounds angry, and yes, my uncle notices.

"Uncle David," I rush forward and hug him. Something I haven't done in a long time. I guess Mr. Gleeson isn't the only one acting strange. "I'm so glad to see you. I don't suppose you have a few minutes to give me a ride home. It's so hot out, and my mother wants some fresh, cold milk."

Shut up, Beatrice!

"Why was the door locked?"

"Oh, I was helping Mr. Gleeson lift some boxes in the back, and he's alone in here today. We're done now." I smile. "A ride home, please?"

He's quiet and looks between us. "Get the milk."

"Thanks!" I say happily and run to get another carton of milk. I can't even remember what happened to the one I was holding when Atilio grabbed me.

As I get another, I look behind me and see Essex watching me. I'm not sure what to make of him.

"Beatrice!" Uncle David calls. "I haven't got all day?" His voice comes closer as Essex fades from view.

"Got it." I turn down the aisle and find Uncle David coming toward me with a panicked Mr. Gleeson trailing behind. "It was nice to see you again, Mr. Gleeson, I'll make sure to stop by more often."

Uncle David grunts and puts a strong hand on my shoulder. "You don't need to shop here anymore, Beatrice." He leads me out of the store and shoves me into the back of his patrol car. My heart races as the door slams shut. I tell myself I can survive this short ride.

I'm helping the Redds get out of town. I'm doing something rebellious. A first. My father will not be happy when he finds out. He won't be happy if anyone tells him what I wore into town either.

Uncle David gets behind the wheel and gives me a long look through the rearview mirror. His eyes make me want to squirm, but I don't. I can't go anywhere anyway.

Instead of heading home, he stops in front of the sheriff's office. I frown. "Why did we stop?"

"I work here. Enjoy the scenery. I'll be back...eventually." He climbs out and enters the office without looking back.

What! The! Hell!

I reach forward and slam the gate between the front and back of the car. I lean back in the seat and kick the door. I can't believe this is happening. My heart is racing as I realize I may be in more trouble than I thought. I must get out of here. Not only am I scared, but it's so hot. The air is stifling. In a panic, my hands slide along the inside of the door, trying to find a way out. I shout in frustration, then scream in terror as a hooded figure appears at the window. I put a hand over my mouth to muffle the scream.

The door opens. "Essex?" I mutter.

He glares. "Go! Now!"

I scuttle out of the car, dragging the stupid milk with me. I don't hang around to find out where Essex went. I crouch down and sneak past the sheriff's office, then dash along the street.

There will be so much trouble when Uncle David finds me gone. I hope no one saw Essex free me.

Sweat soaks my clothes as I run through my yard. My face is flushed, and I feel overheated. Entering the house through the kitchen door, I drop to my knees and roll onto my back. Panting, I give Evelyn—our maid—a thumbs up so she knows I'm okay. I'm in doubt, mind you, because my heart is pounding in my chest.

"What on earth happened, Beatrice? Have you been running in this heat?"

Tears fall. "Uncle David locked me in the back of his police car. I couldn't get out. He left me there." I cry, not caring if Evelyn sees me.

"Oh, dear." She walks away and I hear the faucet turn on and a few seconds later turn off. She crouches down beside me and presses a cold, wet towel over my eyes and forehead. "Calm down and you'll cool off faster."

"I feel like such a baby."

"You are not. What your uncle did was cruel. He knows that confinement in small spaces scares you."

"He parked in front of the sheriff's office." I sit up and move so I'm leaning against a cabinet. "He left me there. It was so hot, and the air conditioning was off. I couldn't get out, Evelyn."

"He obviously came back and set you free."

I shake my head slowly, my eyes holding Evelyn's. "He doesn't know I'm gone yet. At least I don't think he does."

She frowns. "Then—"

I lean forward and put a hand over her mouth. I whisper, "Essex Redd showed up and opened the door."

Her eyes go wide. "Are you sure it was him? I can't tell the younger boys apart."

"I'm sure it was." Wasn't it? He didn't look like someone who would help me. He'd rather stand there and watch me suffer.

"You mustn't mention his name to your parents. I'm not only thinking of him, but also of you."

"Don't worry, I won't mention the Redds at all."

"Good, now why don't you clean up while I pour you an iced tea."

"I'd like that, Evelyn."

As I get to my feet, the older woman pulls me into her arms. "At least you haven't seen the other boys in town. Your daddy would go crazy."

I flinch, which she catches. "I can't tell you. I promised."

"Beatrice, I fear for you if anyone finds out."

"It's okay." I put my arms around her. "I won't see them again, so don't worry.

Chapter Four - Atilio

As soon as my three youngest brothers enter the kitchen, my eyes narrow. They come to a stop. "Which genius opened the door of the cop car and let Beatrice out?" Evelyn had told me the girl thought it was Essex, but he would never do that. My eyes go to Galen.

So, I am surprised when Nico comes out from behind the door and declares, "That genius was me." He grins. "The girl freaked out in the car. It was hot as hell." He shrugs and comes fully into the room. "I grabbed the sweatshirt Essex was wearing earlier and pulled up the hood. Nobody saw me but the girl." He grins. "And she thinks it was Essex."

"You idiot," Essex hisses. "Why the hell did you let her think it was me?"

"It wasn't intentional."

"No one sees or speaks to the girl again," I say. "She's off limits."

"Are you claiming her?" Ridge asks.

"She's the mayor's daughter, and her family runs Mount Sterling. So, no, I am not claiming her. She is young and naive. Stay the hell away from her."

"I was planning to," Essex admits.

"Regardless of this little conversation, I liked Beatrice. It can't be easy for her to have him as a father," Galen says. "She didn't blink an eye when we surrounded her. She helped us get away. She's cool."

Ridge puts an arm around his twin's neck. "My twin likes her." He grins.

"Enough! I don't tell you this often, but I will now. Stay away from her."

These idiots love to mess with me. The thing is, I've learned that if I'm not specific and cover all the bases, they're sneaky, and that doesn't change with age. That's what happens with five brothers.

Mom comes in from the back of the house and as I watch her, I wonder how she survived the six of us.

"What now?" she says.

I subtly shake my head at the idiots. "They set their sights on an unattainable girl, that's all. I told them to stay away."

"Hmm."

"You didn't have to tell me." Essex glares. "Her father killed ours."

Mom gasps knowing who he refers to, a hand to her chest. I jump up and go to her, but Essex is there first. "I'm sorry, but it's true."

"No." She pats Essex's cheeks. "Do not blame Beatrice for her father's misdeeds. Evelyn Park works in the Lincoln Mansion. She adores Beatrice. I won't hear a bad word about her." Mama still has that 'look' that shuts my brother up like nothing else can. "Now leave Atilio alone and clean up the mess you tried to hide in the garage."

Once we're alone, Mom adds, "You should find yourself a nice girl. Someone to take care of you. You took on a lot when your father died. It worries me."

"I found a nice girl today," I add, remembering how Beatrice Lincoln felt when I held her close.

Mom gives me a somber look. "Take your own advice and stay away from the girl. If you go after Beatrice, you will only bring yourself grief. Her family will bring a lot of trouble that none of us can handle."

"I understand that. I was teasing." I get up from the table and kiss Mom on the cheek. She stands and pulls me into her arms. "You're a good son, Atilio."

Mom rarely gets emotional, but when she does, it hits me. I kiss her cheek before pulling away. "I'm going to help them clean up." I pause in the doorway and turn to face her. "Beatrice, why is she so unhappy?"

I surprise her, and worry lines appear on her face. "Atilio," she whispers.

"Please, Mom, tell me."

"She will be married and pregnant within a year, all arranged. The sweet, innocent child is not free to live the life she wants... Please do not look in her direction."

I hold mom's eyes for a while. I want to reassure her that I'll never see Beatrice again, but that's impossible when the girl piques my interest. She showed no fear when I took her in my arms. And the way she ate those popsicles should be illegal. I doubt I'll be the only one having wet dreams about her tonight.

"Don't worry, Mom," I say before heading outside. As I do so, one of my brothers leans against the wall near the kitchen window. I frown, "You heard everything?"

He starts walking toward the garage. "Yeah, I heard. I hope you are planning on listening to Mom." He stomps off.

I grimace and watch Essex go.

Available Now!

MY BROTHER'S GIRL
BAD BOY ROCKERS BOOK 1

Thalia jumps at the chance to spend the summer with her new 'boyfriend' and his family in Alabama. It means she gets to have fun with Liam instead of heading home to her restrictive life. What she hasn't bargained for, is Liam's older brother, Jack—her life suddenly becomes complicated.

Jack gives her sultry glances and touches her heart in a way no one ever has while Liam acts indifferent. No matter what happens this summer, she has to remember to stay away from Jack—however, that becomes impossible when he's everywhere she is.

What is a girl to do?

He has muscle.

He has tattoos.

He has piercings.

He has a mouth a filthy mouth.

He's her boyfriend's older brother.

Available Now!

Chapter One - Thalia

The lumps of the new sofa dug painfully into my back as I wriggled to a new position—equally as uncomfortable as the first. I would never understand how Callie had convinced me to purchase it. I hated it. From the color, a sickly brown—sienna according to the designer—to the numerous lumps and bumps that you couldn't escape, regardless of how you were sitting on it. It reminded me of the old, beat up sofa in my mom's sunroom. The very one my uncle had hauled out and deposited in the tree house we'd built behind the tall cottonwoods.

I smiled at the memory. My first make out session had happened in that tree house, on that sofa. Ethan. Ethan Rock. The school jock and biggest asshole. He'd sweet talked his way into the tree house with every intention of getting to third base. I'd ended up kneeing him in his junk when my father shouted me from the base of the tree. He'd frightened the shit out of us. Ethan, of course hadn't spoken to me again, but what a memory.

"Thalia, what the hell are you grinning at?"

"Ethan Rock," I replied to my roommate Callie, her voice shaking me from the memory.

"Huh, I don't think I know him. You going to eat this Spaghetti Bolognese?"

I turned my head to look at her and burst out laughing. "Is there any left in the pan?" Her apron seemed to have a hell of a lot of red sauce all over it.

Callie was the world's worst chef, and always insisted the next meal she cooked would be better than the previous one. *That was so not going to happen.*

"Ha, funny."

"When's it ready?"

"Ten minutes," she said, before turning back into the small, cramped kitchen.

"Okay." I hoped I wouldn't regret eating what she'd made.

I'd met Callie within a couple of weeks of starting our freshman year at college, both of us studying English Literature—close to three years ago. After the summer break we'd be back as seniors. We couldn't wait to strut our stuff around campus. *Shit, who was I kidding?*

We had it all planned, or at least Callie did. I had no clue as to where I wanted to go, or what I wanted to do, but I figured if I had an English degree, it would open more doors for me, once I'd fully made my mind up.

All I did know was that I wasn't going home when I graduated next year. I shuddered at the thought.

Both of my parents treated me like a child when I was home, right down to the nine pm curfew. I sighed thinking of them. I was twenty-one and, wanted to be like most twenty-one year olds and allowed to enjoy myself before I got completely snowed down with a job and other responsibilities.

Wherever I ended up, I knew that it would be with Callie, although at that thought I realized I'd have to learn to cook if we didn't want to survive on take-out or die from food poisoning.

Dragging my carcass from the sofa, I walked the short distance to the bathroom, which was as small as the kitchen. In the tight space, I could touch the toilet, washbasin and shower and feel cramped in doing so. There was barely enough room at the sink to wash up for dinner.

Rent was cheap so I guess I shouldn't complain too much. My parents gave me a monthly allowance that covered the rent, bills and food. I even had some left over, which I put away for rainy days or when I'd finished school, along with the money from my part-time job.

I sighed, turning the faucet on, I splashed cold water onto my face. Green eyes returned my gaze in the mirror. Groaning, I realized my dark curly hair, which had been secured in a band at the back of my head, had come loose. Stray hairs were sticking up all over my head in disarray. I pulled the towel from the rail and dried my face, with an extra swipe over my freckled nose, in hope that one or two freckles would get stuck on the towel. *I hated freckles!* My red hairbrush was in the container to the side of the tub, so I quickly grabbed it, removed the band from my hair, and ran the brush through it, deciding to leave it hanging around my shoulders.

Refreshed, I walked into the kitchen, and took a seat at our two-person table while Callie spooned sauce on to the pasta.

She placed the plate in front of me and I couldn't hold the grimace in as the sharp odor of unknown spices drifted from the plate. *Oh boy.*

"Thalia, I promise it's tasty," she reassured me between bites. "Are you for real?"

"Okay, I'm hungry so here goes." I picked up my

fork, rolled up the long noodles dripping with sauce and placed it hesitantly into my mouth. Flavor burst on my tongue and to my surprise it was edible! I glanced at Callie in surprise.

"Told you so." She smirked.

"What happened? Why does it taste good?" That's the thing about best friends—you could insult them without it going to heart. Callie was also honest with herself and knew she couldn't cook.

"Well, thanks for the vote of confidence. I kept telling you I'd get it right one of these days," Callie replied, waving her fork around in the air.

"Yeah, you did and watch what you're doing with that fork."

We ate the rest of the meal in silence then I poured us both a glass of wine, which we carried through to the living room along with the rest of the bottle. We got comfortable on the sofa with our feet resting up on the coffee table, the conversation and wine flowing easily between us. Before we knew it we were on our second bottle of wine.

"So who's Ethan Rock?"

I frowned at her. "It took you long enough to ask."

"You still haven't answered."

"Ethan Rock was the school jock, aka school asshole, who tried to get to third base in my tree house. It was cut short by my dad calling upto me," I giggled. "I kneed him in the junk. He ended up rolling all over the floor in his shorts while I tried to hold a conversation with my dad without laughing. Ethan never spoke to me again."

"Oh my God. How old were you?"

"Sweet sixteen," I replied, starting to feel the effects of drinking nearly two bottles of wine with Callie.

"Nothing sweet about what you nearly did." We fell into each other laughing.

After picking ourselves up from the floor, I walked into the kitchen for more wine and the cake I'd brought home with me from work.

"Here, share this with me." I passed Callie a slice before sitting back down beside her.

"Why didn't I get the job in the cake shop instead of the dry cleaners?"

"Because you have a sweet tooth. You're skinny now. If you'd taken the job with the cakes you wouldn't be able to walk through the door," I teased my sulking friend.

"I thought you were my friend."

"I am. That's why I work in the cake shop and you don't," I laughed.

We both hated our jobs, which we considered slave labor, although I did have the slightly better one in the cake shop. Unfortunately, today had been my last day. The cake shop was on campus, and only opened during the college semesters, whereas the dry cleaners where Callie worked were open twenty-four-seven, much to Callie's constant dismay.

"Before you get too drunk to think, I want to know what's going on between you and Liam, and don't tell me nothing."

I digested Callie's question. How could I answer when, in actual fact, I had no idea? Over the past six months we'd been on a few dates and to the movies once or twice, but there was something missing. In honesty, I think if I hadn't been so busy with my studies I would have said something to him, about the lack of closeness between us. He hadn't even kissed me, other than a peck on the cheek. Liam was good company and rather entertaining so I'd just gone along with him as his 'girlfriend.'

Callie was staring at me with the patience of a saint. Her long legs rested beside mine on the coffee table and she was slouched on the couch. Her eyes half closed in a lazy manner, blonde hair falling in disarray from the 'up do' she had going on from the morning.

"Liam is good looking, but he hasn't tried to get into my pants. Not even once. He's kissed me, kind of, but no other touching." I hesitated before blurting out, "I'm going home with him this summer."

Callie choked on the swallow of wine she'd just taken, the red liquid staining her white top as her eyes widened in shock. "Are you crazy?"

"Probably," I groaned.

Callie dabbed at her shirt as she stared at me looking flabbergasted.

"Look, you know I don't want to go home." I numbered out the reasons on my fingers. "All the summer jobs around here have already been taken. You're going away with your family, and I don't want to touch my savings. I can use some, but the majority I want to save. You know that."

I avoided her gaze as I reaffirmed all my reasons for going. "Liam said his parents want him to bring me home. He also said, I'll have my own room, and I do like him, but as a friend. To be honest I think that's what he wants, although he keeps referring to me as his girlfriend." I frowned.

"This can only end in disaster." Callie sat up, her gaze serious. "What are you going to do if this is all a ruse to finally get in your panties? Because I can tell you're not into him like that. Though I doubt you ever were to begin with," Callie finished, truth ringing in her words.

"Then I'll deal with it, if, or when that happens," I muttered.

Callie's hard gaze bore into me, making me shift uncomfortably under it before she stifled a yawn with the back of her hand. "I need to get some sleep and don't forget we're going shopping in the morning," she reminded me as she struggled up from the sofa and stumbled into her room.

Despite her warnings, I was looking forward to going home with Liam, although I was a bit apprehensive about meeting his parents. Hopefully I'd meet a *HOT* cowboy there. *They had cowboys in Alabama, right?*

I pulled myself up from the sofa and headed to my room where I collapsed on top of my bed. I was so tired.

Both Callie and I were still suffering the effects from last night's wine drinking. Callie had been sick and I'd woken up with drums beating in my head. I'd taken some painkillers about an hour ago so the drum in my head had dimmed enough that I'd stopped feeling sick, which was just as well because we were in one of Callie's favorite stores trying on dresses.

I'd bought a pair of cowgirl boots about six months ago on a trip home with Callie to Texas for her parent's thirtieth wedding anniversary, and I loved them. They were authentic cowgirl boots from Allen's Boots in Austin, in soft, light brown leather. Deep brown, embroidered poppies decorated the boots making them the perfect accessory for any event. They'd set me back a bit, but I'd always wanted a pair and they were so worth it.

All I wanted were some dresses to wear them with. You see, I had it in my head that I was going to fall head over heels in love with a cowboy, but I'd worked out that 'said cowboy' had to fall in love with me too, hence the dresses to go with the boots. I mean what guy could resist a woman in cowgirl boots and a short dress? Flashing naked thighs!

As I wiggled into the third dress, music started blaring from somewhere close by. *Oh my God!* Where the hell was that racket coming from? My head was about to explode.

I could hear Callie groaning in the changing room beside mine. "Thalia, answer your *goddamn* phone," she shouted.

It was me? *Shit*. My fogged brain hadn't registered the fact. I grabbed my jeans from the floor where I'd thrown them in my haste to try on the white lacy dress, and quickly retrieved my iPhone from the back pocket. My stomach rolled with nausea, so after taking some deep breaths, I answered, which cut off one of my favorite songs, '*Here Without You*' by Three Doors Down.

"Hello." I slid to the floor, shutting my eyes, praying that everything stopped spinning.

"Thalia, dear. Is that you?"

"Mom," I groaned, just what I needed, a lecture when I was still feeling the effects of too much red wine from the night before. "Yes, it's me."

"I just wanted to know when you're going to arrive home for the summer. We need to make plans."

"Mom, about that." I took a deep breath, mentally bracing myself. "I'm not going to be coming home. I've been invited to a friend's home in Alabama for the summer. So, having never been to Alabama before, I've accepted. I mean it's not as though you and Dad will be there all the time, you both usually head out on a cruise." I crossed my fingers.

"Well! Do we know this person who you prefer over your own parents?"

Ugh. Why did she always have to make me feel guilty? "No you don't know him." The silence on the phone was icy. I sighed before continuing, "His name is Liam. His father has a law firm which he jointly owns with another guy, so totally trustworthy."

"Now Thalia, lawyers are not trustworthy, they're sharks."

Here we go again. All because one lawyer swindled Mom and Dad out of a load of money, they're all sharks!

"Mom, I don't want to argue. His parents are already expecting me, and I'm sorry for not telling you sooner. I'll come and visit before I head back here to school, okay?"

"Look after yourself, Thalia. I'll email you our schedule. Please make sure you email your contact details for Alabama." She hung up.

I rested my head against the wall of the changing room staring at the phone. No goodbye, the guilt trip had been minor for my mom. Sighing in relief, I realized the spinning in my head had stopped, and I felt much better having spoken to my mom, a conversation that I'd been putting off.

"Thalia, you alive in there?" Callie banged on the door.

"Yeah! Give me a minute." I removed the dress and decided to take all five, even though I'd only tried on three of them. There was a mixture of colors: white, cream, pale lemon, pale green and pale lilac. Yeah, I liked pale colors.

My jeans were in a heap on the floor so I picked them up, shook them out before I wiggled back into them. I gathered the dresses together and left the changing rooms in search of Callie. As it turned out I didn't have far to look. She stood talking to Liam outside the door to the changing rooms.

"Hey, Thalia." He leaned forward, kissing me on the cheek. "Let me take those. You both finished here? I thought I'd take you and Callie to lunch."

Liam took the bundle of dresses from me so I took his arm and let him lead me to the check out. "Lunch would be great, now that my hangover has more or less disappeared."

"Hangover? I thought you said you were staying in last night," Liam queried.

"Wine night at our apartment," I replied.

"Okay. You buying all these?" Liam asked as he placed them onto the cashier desk.

"Yeah. I don't have that many dresses, so I figured I'd add to my wardrobe as I'm going home with you." I handed my charge card over to the sales assistant and turned to Callie. "What happened to the dress you had?"

"I've changed my mind. I'm going to leave you two. I have some things to do before I head in to work in a couple of hours." Callie started to back away from us.

"You sure?"

"Positive. I'd probably puke anyway." She turned and headed out the store.

Liam took hold of the bags with my dresses and ushered me out of the store to a new café that had opened across the road.

I had slight misgivings about going home with Liam this summer. He—us—confused me. Was I his girlfriend or just a friend? He was gorgeous in so many ways. Tall, slim but still athletic and his blonde hair and blue eyes gave him the appearance of the All American Boy. All the girls on campus wanted his attention, but for some reason he was interested in me.

As I admitted to Callie last night, we hadn't gotten to the hot and sweaty part of dating yet, and I wasn't too sure I wanted to. We got along fairly well, but I didn't get all hot and bothered in his presence. No tingles or wet panties. Even walking beside him, all I felt was the warmth of friendship.

Standing outside the Italian café in the sweltering heat we scanned the menu in the hopes that they had something worth eating. "Ah." I slid my finger past the list of sandwiches and brought it to rest on the lasagna and garlic bread—just what I wanted.

Liam glanced over my finger and grinned, "You are feeling better if you're looking at that."

"I'm hungry now. What about you?" I grinned.

"I think I'll have the same. Come on, let's go and order."

Liam opened the door for me and we stepped into the dim interior. A maître'd cleared his throat before he led us to the terrace out back, sitting us in the shade.

We placed our order with the server and sat back to relax while I let the breeze cool my skin. The café hadn't been open long, so everything still looked new and fresh. Our table was beside the garden, which had a manmade stream flowing through, with brightly colored flowers along both sides of the embankment. How they'd managed to create a beautiful garden oasis in the middle of the city was beyond me.

I glanced at Liam. "Will you tell me more about your family? What to expect?"

He laughed. "It might scare you off if I do."

"They can't be as bad as my parents."

"Not really. I guess." Liam knew all about my parents. He took a sip of his water and peered at me, his blue eyes sparkling in mirth. He was obviously enjoying this. "Okay. My father is a lawyer and has his own law practice, which he jointly owns with an old friend of his, Lewis. My older brother, Jack is engaged to marry Lewis's daughter, Mia."

"I didn't know you had a brother." Surprise turned to confusion. Why hadn't he told me before? We'd had the sibling conversation during one of our earlier dates. If that's what you'd call them, and he never mentioned a brother.

"Yeah. They're getting married over the summer, Jack's twenty-five, and studying to be a lawyer. He's been groomed since we were kids to take our father's place at the law firm. Dad wants him to settle into life as a family lawyer, whereas Jack has always held a fascination in criminal law. He's the golden boy because he's studying law," he sneered.

"I take it you don't get along too well with him?"

"We get along well enough or at least we used to do. He seems angry all the time."

God, did I want to head to Alabama? Yeah, I did—one word—*cowboys*. Besides, I liked weddings. I'd had the pleasure of being a bridesmaid at twelve weddings in my twenty-one years, so it would be fun to go to one in Alabama.

"Thalia, let's eat and talk about something else. My stomach can't take anymore talk about my family."

Chapter Two - Thalia

In the process of trying to pull my skinny jeans up my legs, Callie came barging into my room with a brush stuck in her hair. The 'stuck brush' happened nearly every time we were getting ready to go out, often because she was trying to multi task. Multi tasking wasn't exactly something Callie was capable of, probably why she was a bit hit-and-miss with cooking.

With my jeans finally up around my hips, I left them unbuttoned to try and untangle the brush.

"How do you always manage to get this thing tangled?"

"*Ouch!*"

"Sorry," I said grinning as my fingers worked the mess of hair through the brush.

"I keep thinking about having it all cut off, but it wouldn't be me, you know?"

"Yeah, I know. Just try and remember to concentrate when you're doing your hair in the future, because one of these days you're going to end up having to have the brush cut out."

Slapping the now free brush into Callie's hand, I laughed as she jumped up from my bed and ran back into her room.

Tonight was our last night together until the end of the summer when we came back to our apartment to finish our final year of college. Oh, we'd be on the phone to each other, and maybe try to meet up at some point, but it wasn't the same. I would miss Callie.

While I'd been packing my clothes and accessories during the afternoon, I had second thoughts about going home with Liam. I liked him well enough, but after hearing about his family and his brother, I couldn't shake the lump of worry that had settled in the pit of my stomach.

"Thalia, you ready," Callie shouted as she poked her head into my room. "What's wrong?"

I inhaled. "Nothing. Come on lets go." I ushered her through our small apartment, grabbing our jackets and purses on the way out, before she could question me further.

Once outside, I had to dash to keep up with her. Deciding that the night would go smoother with a few rules, I said, "I'm not drinking too much tonight. I have a long car journey tomorrow, so I don't want to be puking all the way there. I also wouldn't put it past Liam to leave me if I get sick in his car."

She stopped and turned, a worry line traced its way across her forehead as her gaze bored into me. "I think you're making a mistake," her tone was clipped as though she was holding back, "but it's your decision." She frowned as I tugged her arm to get her moving again instead of replying right away.

I loved her like a sister, but I had to make my own decisions. If I didn't, Callie would end up treating me like a little girl, just like my parents did. "I'm a big girl now." I smiled to take the challenge out of my tone. "If I'm not happy there then I'll head home, or to Texas."

"You promise."

"Yes Mom," I laughed, pushing my way through the door of Luke's as Callie followed me inside.

Luke's was a five-minute walk from where we lived, and every Friday night they had a live band. More often than not it was 'The Leopards,' not sure where that name came from, but they were good. Luke's always had a full house when they played.

We pushed our way through the crush of bodies to the bar. The eyes of some college guys tracked us like prey, which I guess single college girls were. I ignored the interested looks. Other college girls might not mind being prey, but Callie and I did. The guys in here knew to leave us alone, but a few couldn't take no for an answer.

Callie and I weren't opposed to being hit on, I mean what girl doesn't like a hot guy flirting with her, but after putting up with it for nearly three years, it kind of sucked.

Standing at the bar, I spotted some friends on the dance floor so, after Callie passed me a beer, we headed toward them. We loved to dance and during the past six months had only allowed ourselves to let go once a month, due to the papers we had to get written before the end of the semester, plus, of course, there were our jobs. Our jobs being another reason why I hadn't been too bothered about Liam's lack of passion. It had been so long since I'd felt like a normal twenty-one year old.

"Hey," Jeff whispered into my ear, his arms wrapping around my waist as he snuggled in against my back. Jeff was harmless and totally not into me. As in, he much preferred someone with a dick! Callie and I were the only ones who knew that because we'd once seen him kissing a guy. We'd basically been in the wrong place at the wrong time. We'd become friends, and now and again I would go out with him and let everyone think we were dating to help him keep his secret. He was a good sounding board and had let me rant about my family and guys, more often than I'd care to admit.

Jeff pushed me further onto the dance floor with him. Keeping his hands on my hips he started swaying to a slow song that had come on. He was only a couple of inches taller than my five-foot-six frame so he was pretty easy to dance with.

The Leopards usually played the slow song before they took a break, so any minute I expected the speaker system to kick in with 'Panic! At the Disco,' which was pretty good, or something else as Mick was the bar tender tonight and he loved the kind of music that had a bite to it. I was one hundred percent into Three Doors Down, which drove Callie mad, as she was more Taylor Swift and Carrie Underwood. I'd yet to admit to liking them as well.

On my second bottle of beer, thanks to Callie, I continued to dance and grind against Jeff who wasn't affected one bit with my ass rubbing against his dick.

I placed my empty bottle onto a table at the side of the dance floor, before I practically threw myself into Jeff's arms as we started jumping and singing along to 'The Leopards'.

After about an hour on the dance floor with Jeff, I turned to him and shook my head, to let him know I needed a break. Leaving him alone, I walked toward the table where Callie was sitting with Chase, David, Liam, Nadine and Kristy—some friends we occasionally hooked up with.

Liam made room for me, so I slid into the seat. "You looked good out there," he shouted, kissing me smack on the lips.

My eyes flew wide open. Callie looked about as stunned as I felt. That was new. Liam had never shown me any affection in public before. Narrowing my eyes, I took his challenge. I turned in his embrace and straddled him, wrapping my arms around his neck and plunged in. I needed to see if there was anything between us once and for all. I put my all into it and maybe we had potential, because my blood started to tingle and Liam started to grow between my legs. I pressed against him. Liam broke the kiss and just looked at me.

"God, you're hot tonight," Liam commented.

Our breathing was labored while we continued to stare at each other in shock, in truth I felt confused. Liam was great to hang out with and we had been dating, kind of, for the past six months, but we hadn't kissed like that before.

"Wow, you two looked ready to get down and dirty," Kristy said as Liam moved me from his lap with unsteady hands.

"Thalia, do you want to leave?"

I hesitated at Liam's question.

"I don't mean to follow up with more than a kiss. I just meant because we have an early start tomorrow." Liam practically had to shout in my ear to be heard.

"Okay." We stood to leave, the others giving us knowing looks, but Callie knew me better than anyone else and knew Liam wouldn't be spending time in my bed.

I leaned over to shout in Callie's ear, "Are you coming or staying?"

"Staying. I'll get Jeff to walk me back."

We hugged, and then I let Liam pull me through the crowd to the outside. It was good to breathe fresh air after being squished in the sweaty bar.

Liam grasped my hand, his grip sending tendrils of warmth up my arm while we walked back to my apartment in silence. He appeared to be as lost in thought as I was. He was probably replaying the kiss. The kiss, which had come out of the blue. Could I blame it on the alcohol? Probably not. He knew I'd only had two beers. The kiss had been hot. He certainly knew how to kiss.

"Are you okay? You've been quiet since we left the bar." His tone seemed unsure, but I couldn't tell what he was unsure about.

I reached up and touched along my tender lips with my fingers. His eyes narrowed as he watched me. "I was thinking," I met his eyes, "can we try that again?"

He shook his head, about to say something, but I didn't give him time. I stepped into his space, took hold of his head, pulled him down to me, and sealed our lips together. I wanted to know if the kiss and reaction at the bar was a one off.

Our lips met. Our bodies touched, chest to chest and, nothing. It was nice, but, nothing. I slowly pulled back and looked into Liam's eyes. He looked flushed.

"Thalia." He reached up and brushed the hair away from my face. "I'm not ready to become intimate with you. I like you a lot and I can talk to you. I guess I'm afraid of losing that if we hit the sack. You know what I mean?"

"I'd like that—a lot." I nearly laughed out loud when I saw the look on his face. He looked as relieved as me.

"When I take you home tomorrow, would it be okay for me to tell everyone that you're my girl-friend? I mean we may end up together anyway. It would just stop my mom from constantly parading girls through the house," he asked, looking hesitant.

"Okay, I guess." I glanced up to the dark window of my apartment, "I better head upstairs." I turned away and started to open the front door.

"Thanks Thalia, you're great." He came up behind me, kissing me on the cheek before stepping back. I watched him turn back toward Luke's for his car.

"Goodnight Liam, I'll see you bright and early."

"That you will. Goodnight Thalia."

Chapter Three - Jack

Saturday night and I was knocking back a beer before it was Deception's turn on stage. I lived for these nights. Deception being the group I'd started back in high school with a couple of friends. Reece was on the drums, while Donovan worked his electric guitar, which left me to sing solo, occasionally bringing my guitar out.

Deception was also one of my big secrets. As far as my parents were concerned the 'band phase' had come to an end when we all left high school. Little did they know!

I had another year of hard studying to do before I could get out from under them. It was going to be a hard year, not just because of the studying. I was going to piss good old dad off when he found out my program at college would be all geared to me practicing criminal law. All I had to do was get through the summer before I headed back to school. *A married man—Fuck!*

Kix had been open a couple of months and for the past couple of weeks, since we'd arrived home from school, Reece, Donovan and me had played on stage about three times. After our first appearance, people had been asking when we were coming back. Deciding it was a great way to spend the summer, we'd struck a deal with Ryder, and now we wanted to extend the deal to maybe a Wednesday night as well as the Saturday spot we already had. Ryder wanted to think about it.

"You seen the chick over there?" Reece asked, pointing his bottle of beer in the direction of the blonde girl who looked to have melons for breasts.

"Not interested." The thing was I hadn't been interested in close to twelve months, ever since I had Mia thrust on me. Mia my fiancée, the woman I was being faithful to. The woman I didn't want, but was trapped with.

"You need a distraction my friend, and that over there, is a distraction."

"*Fuck.* Reece, I am so not going there. If you're that interested, you go for it."

After a minute of silence from me, he grabbed another beer and walked toward the 'chick.' What my friends couldn't understand was why I stayed faithful to someone I didn't love and didn't like spending time with. I may have allowed my family to push me into marriage, which would happen in about six weeks, but I wouldn't cheat on the girl. I'd tried to tell my folks I wanted to wait until after school before I committed myself to her. I hoped she'd have changed her mind by then so I'd be off the hook. For some reason everyone, including my so-called fiancée, wanted the wedding this summer.

I'd returned home from school to find the wedding arranged and to be told, all I had to do was show up. To say I'd gotten totally and utterly drunk that night would be an understatement.

Why did I let my parents push me into a wedding I didn't want? Well, I was so close to finishing school and my father had put my financial future on the line. I'd studied damn hard so the last thing I wanted to do was pull from the program.

I tried not to think about it too much, and just hoped everything, including my feelings, fell into place.

Looking at other women was out of the question, because I was frightened that if I did, I might find the woman I'd been looking for before my life got 'arranged.' The one that I'd dreamed about. Regardless of what my friends thought, before my life had taken a turn, I would have loved nothing more than to find the woman meant for me. Instead of the constant stream of women gracing my sheets, I'd just have the one woman.

"I see he's found some company," Donovan pointed out.

"I'm surprised you're not with him," I stated, turning away from Reece's flirting and looked at Donovan who was in his usual black jeans and white t-shirt, which was stretched tight over his abs. He'd been my friend for about thirteen years, and he knew me better than my own family did. Usually he'd go in for the kill with Reece, even if it was just the one woman.

"Maybe later. We're up in a minute." Donovan turned and leaned against the bar. "We have a good crowd here tonight. Do you think they'd come and watch us on a Wednesday as well?"

We surveyed the bodies, which were packed tightly into the place, here to let off steam to our music. It felt damn good knowing they were here because of us.

"Yeah, I do. Maybe not as many, but I guess the majority of them would. The only problem I might have is work." I took a long swallow of beer, grimacing at the thought of spending the summer under my dad's watchful eyes. It had been my idea so I couldn't complain too much. "I can shift things around and work when I get home if I have to. I really want the Wednesday slot." I drained the rest of my beer knowing I needed our music to get me through the week.

I still dreamed of having a life of my choosing, but six weeks would be here all too soon and it took all my strength to stay strong.

"Hey," Donovan nudged me with his beer.

"What?"

"What?" Donovan repeated. "Where'd you go?"

"Thinking about the shit I have to look forward too," I replied with a heavy sigh.

"Talking about shit, isn't your brother home tomorrow?"

I laughed, because neither, Donovan or Reece got along with Liam and vice-versa. "Yeah, he is and apparently he's bringing his girl with him."

Donovan spat his mouth full of beer out, luckily onto the floor and not me. "You fucking with me?"

I held my hands out. "Nope, he is. Moms been sprucing the place up, driving me crazy, following me around making sure I didn't just dump my boots at the foot of the stairs. Trust me, I tried and within five minutes, they came flying in my room, with the door banging shut behind her. *God*, she's driving me nuts."

"She always drives you nuts," Reece pointed out, reappearing—*alone*. "They're ready for us. Which song do you want to kick off with?"

"Hero." I'd written the song myself and it was loud with a bite to it. The crowd usually went wild when we sang it, especially when Reece lost his t-shirt toward the end, flashing his tattoos not to mention his muscles.

"Okay, let's bring this place to life," Reece said, walking in the direction of the stage. "You girls coming," he asked Donovan and me when we made no move to follow him.

We finally started to follow Reece as Ryder climbed on to the stage.

"Okay y'all, shut the fuck up," came blaring through the speakers. Not one to mix words was Ryder, a thirty-year-old ex-marine with a bad attitude, who just happened to own the bar and for some reason liked us.

"I know y'all are here to see my smiling face." Half the crowd laughed and the other half whistled. "Sorry to disappoint y'all, but you're going to have to put up with Deception." With that he leapt from the stage as we climbed up on it.

As I placed the mic back into the stand, I couldn't help but smile in pride. We rocked the place tonight and even ended our turn on stage with 'Love, Lost and Found.' It was a slow number to give the guys in the crowd a chance to get their hands on the women.

While I'd been singing, I'd had a front row seat watching the 'chick' from before going between the three of us with lust clear in her eyes. She had no chance with me, but I'd glanced at Donovan and Reece a few times and knew as soon as our stint was over they'd be all over her, and in her.

I'd be a liar if I said I hadn't been turned on with the sizzling glances she'd kept throwing at me, because I had been. The boner in my jeans could attest to that. Unfortunately, I couldn't act on it.

Walking toward the bar to distract myself from the throbbing going on below my belt, I bumped into a dark haired girl, who started to tumble forwards.

Placing my hands on her hips to stop her from tipping over, her ass rubbed up against my groin.

She turned her head. "Is that for me?" she purred, rubbing against my dick, which had gone hard as fuck.

Taking a deep breath, I gently pushed her away from me, "No. Sorry."

I carried on walking, but changed direction toward the back where I knew the guys had taken the 'chick.' God, I hated that word. I needed to come badly, otherwise my dick wouldn't go down. I hadn't had sex in forever, but my fist worked fine, although I was getting fed up with it.

Donovan and Reece were in the storeroom, so taking another breath, I knocked on the door. "Guys, it's me," I shouted through the door, knowing it would be useless trying to open it since it would be locked.

I heard the lock click before the door opened slightly. I pushed my way in, much to Donovan's shock.

"You're joining us?" Reece asked, in disbelief from between the woman's thighs.

"Not exactly." I wasn't sure what the hell I was doing in the room with them. Sex was out of the question because since Mia I'd stopped with the one-night stands. Once or twice I'd watched the guys with women, jerking off to the show.

This wasn't a first. We'd done a threesome with a woman on more than one occasion with our cocks in her cunt, ass and mouth. Yeah, it had been hot as fuck, and with just the memory, my dick hardened even more.

"I'm staying over here," I said, backing up to the wall, resting against it. I had a first class view of the naked woman on the desk, who was already groaning, thrashing her head from side to side. I wasn't surprised as Reece had his mouth buried between her thighs. Donovan sucked her tits and then she came with a squeal, which Donovan moved to capture in his mouth.

I stroked my cock through my jeans, then thought *fuck it*, unzipped and unbuttoned the denim that had been keeping me contained and let my swollen dick burst free.

Both Reece and Donovan had their cocks out now and had suited up. Donovan was standing to the side of her, his junk level with her face, while she lapped at his balls like there was no tomorrow.

Taking hold of my cock, I started to move my

hand back and forth, rubbing the wet tip with my thumb. *Christ it felt good.* What I really wanted to do was walk over to her and soak my cock in her cunt juice.

Fuck, I slammed my head back against the wall. Through heavy lidded eyes, seconds from coming, I watched as Reece thrust into the woman's wet sex, rubbing her clit with his fingers, while Donovan fucked her mouth, squeezing her nipples between his thumb and finger.

I knew the three of us were ready to blow, but we waited for the woman.

Reece leaned over her while slamming into her like a fucking train, knocked one of Donovan's hands from her tit, and started to suck her nipple. She came apart under him.

Donovan started to come, followed by Reece, as they brought the woman up and over again, triggering my release.

Biting my lip, I came all over the bottom of my fucking t-shirt, which I'd used to cover the tip of my cock, just before I blew. Coming back to my senses, I whipped the t-shirt off and cleaned up, before shoving everything back inside my jeans.

Standing against the wall, I watched them dress

the woman, who had a glazed, just been fucked, look on her face. As they walked her to the door, they took it in turns to kiss her, before patting her on the ass and sending her through the open door.

Closing the door with grins on their faces, they both looked at me, and for once I was glad of the darkness where I stood, because I was slightly embarrassed, and probably blushed like a fucking girl.

"Don't say a word," I told them, as I walked out the room, slamming the door behind me.

It was late, but after jerking off to the show Donovan and Reece put on with the woman, who Donovan informed me was named Simone, in the backroom of Kix, I felt restless as hell. I thought I'd feel better after releasing the tension that gripped me, but no such luck. In fact, I felt worse than before.

When our stint was over with, we'd loaded Donovan's car with our gear, and then driven back to his place to chill for a while. I needed a place to relax before I could face going home.

"Here," Donovan pressed a bottle of beer into my

hand. I took a deep drink from the longneck before stretching out on his porch.

Both my best friends were lounging around with me, but it was Reece's gaze that was starting to bug me.

I turned my head full on to return his stare. "What?"

"It's been a while since all three of us have done anything like we did tonight. You should have joined in more. She tasted fucking good. She'd rubbed some strawberry stuff over her pussy." Reece smacked his lips together.

I groaned remembering what it was like to go down on a woman, which was a bad idea considering what that image was doing to my dick.

"How long's it been since you got your dick wet? Twelve months? I'm telling you, get rid of Mia and break the dry spell. God, Simone's cunt was so fucking wet and tight."

Glaring daggers at Reece, I willed him to shut the fuck up. My dick was hard as a fucking spike again and there was nothing I could do for it. By the look of things, Reece and Donovan weren't faring any better.

"You're a bastard," I informed him.

"Just wanted you to know what you missed."

"I could see real well from where I was standing."

"Watching her little mouth wrap around my cock with bright red lips was such a turn-on," Donovan added, laughing when he glanced at my groin.

The bastards knew what they were doing to me, but at least they'd gotten boners as well.

I inhaled, counted to ten then exhaled. *"Fuckers."*

With that being said, I stood and walked to my car, retrieved my guitar with Reece and Donovan walking up behind me, their chuckles of amusement filling the air.

Ignoring them, I walked back to the porch, lifted my guitar from its case and started moving my fingers over the strings, wanting the guys to hear what I'd done so far with the new song I'd been working on, 'Tonight.'

Donovan was the first to break the silence, following the last note I'd strung. "Wow."

"Fucking awesome," Reece commented, sitting beside me with his guitar. "Play it again without the lyrics." Reece had a talent. One I wished I had. He only had to hear music, and within ten minutes he'd be able to repeat it, flawlessly.

Now available for all online retailers.

LOVE STRYKER
MMA ROMANCE

When my childhood friend, Cora, dared me to write a sexy novel about a martial arts fighter, I agreed, albeit under the influence of alcohol. It was something for me—something different and exciting.

It was supposed to be research, pure and simple. But then I met him—a six-foot-six mountain of a man with no name. The way his muscles flexed and rippled when he trained made my belly quiver. The way his dark hair flopped over his forehead made me want to brush it back from his strong face. His nose had been broken, but it made no difference, he was still a handsome man. He had eyes dark as the night that would land on me the minute I entered his gym…Every…Time.

He was their star fighter, the one that brought in the big money. At first I feared him because of his size and the way he would look at me. But then I discovered that I was his biggest distraction, and no matter what my head told me, my heart told me to fight for the man who didn't know how to live outside of the cage.

NYT & USA Today bestselling author Lexi Buchanan brings you her new sexy standalone novel about fighting for freedom when the odds are against you.

LOVE STRYKER
EXCERPT

Stryker (10 years ago)

"DAD, I'M NOT SURE this is such a good idea." My heart raced in my chest as though it would explode. My palms went slick as fear coursed through my veins.

I'd already thought Dad's late night plans were a bad idea…and they seemed worse the minute I saw the dark, deserted alley. It gave me the chills.

Nothing good was up that alley.

Even at fourteen I knew it, but my dad was determined so I followed him across the street. Something shouted for me to run, which gave me pause, but my legs had a mind of their own and followed him.

My dad turned, and then frowned when he noticed the slight hesitation in my usual eagerness to follow him anywhere. The nervous twitch in his right eye went crazy. "It isn't, but it's the only thing I can do."

Before I could work out what he meant, my dad grabbed my arm as though he was afraid I'd run. He dragged me to the mouth of what I considered a nightmare.

The stench of rotten food made me want to hurl. Every creak, even the wind howling around us, had my eyes constantly straining to see through the pitch black. I half expected someone to jump out brandishing a gun, or knife, or some other weapon.

Head down, my eyes landed on the hold my dad had on my arm. Something wasn't right. In fact, nothing about the evening felt right.

I knew my dad constantly bet on the fighters in the cage, winning and losing on a regular basis, but what that had to do with tonight, if anything, I didn't know. My dad never took me to the fights no matter how much I begged. I wanted to hang out with dad… wanted to be like the fighters—tough, strong, fearless. One day, that would be me standing in the cage with the crowds shouting my name. Then my dad wouldn't have any choice about keeping me away from that life.

I'd never understood the obsession my dad had for the fights, but they'd put him on a high for days afterwards…unless he lost.

Pulled to a stop, I felt the shake of my dad's hand as his grip tightened. He turned to look at me and the fear I saw in his eyes was something I'd never expected to see. My blood turned to ice and the wrongfulness of the night felt all too real as a large vehicle headed down the alley from the opposite entrance.

Caught in the headlights, my first reaction was to run and hide. The tension jumping off my dad was high. His breathing was frantic and sweat beaded on his forehead.

With my free hand, I shoved the black hood of my sweatshirt from my head so I didn't miss anything.

My pulse hammered in my neck and all I could hear was my heartbeat thrashing in my ears.

When my dad's only reaction was to stand and stare at the approaching vehicle, I knew then, that they where here because of him.

What had he done?

"Dad?" I turned and hoped he'd offer me an explanation as fear and anger knotted in my gut.

He didn't and wouldn't meet my gaze until the purr of the SUV's engine cut off. "Son, I'm sorry. If there was any other way I'd have taken it, but there isn't…I love you. You won't believe those words soon, but I mean them with every breath I take."

"What?"

Before he could say more, the doors of the SUV opened and a large man climbed out, moving behind us. Three other men emerged and stood in front.

The one in a dark suit stepped forward, his steely eyes on my dad. "Peter."

"Mr—"

"No names tonight…*Peter.*" His gaze slid to me and my breath caught at the back of my throat. He looked me over—assessing. "He'll do."

What did he mean?

"Dad?"

My dad didn't explain and, seconds later, I felt his grip on my arm loosen as the large guy stepped closer.

None of this made any sense, but I'd known something was wrong the minute I'd stepped out of our apartment.

It was obvious that my dad had done, said, or agreed to something, but my brain worked overtime trying to work out just what.

Then I felt my wrists clasped tightly before they were pulled behind my back in a grip so strong that I knew even as I struggled that I wouldn't get free.

"Dad," I shouted, my eyes begged him to help me, but he just watched while they dragged me away.

The suit held his hand out and halted the guy who had me. He spoke with a threat inflected into his voice to my dad, "With this exchange, you can consider your debt paid in full. You stay away from him and me, and, you never step foot near the cage again…in any city. You won't like the consequences if you do." The man in the dark suit stepped in close to my dad, and threatened, "Am I clear?"

My dad's body quivered in fear and his eyes nearly bugged out of his head while the man threatened him.

Fear trickled from my belly and gradually spread throughout the more I listened to the conversation around me.

Until now, I had no idea just how serious my dad's gambling habit had become. I should have though. But surely he wasn't giving me over to the men to settle his debt. Was he? What did they want with me?

What... No!

The hold on me tightened as I started to struggle. The man behind me wasn't like the others. He was big and strong, and wore jeans and shirt as opposed to the others in suits. His scent was trouble, and even though I continued to struggle, I knew that he wouldn't release me.

My heart pounded as sweat ran down my face, mingling with the tears I couldn't control as my situation sank into my brain.

My dad, who I loved, who I thought loved me, had sold me in exchange for his gambling debt to be wiped clean. How could he do that?

My dad glanced at me one last time, pain in his eyes, before he turned and ran down the alley.

The man behind, tugged me toward a black SUV, but I struggled and tried to dig in my heels, my eyes still on my dad as he ran and left me with these assholes.

At the SUV, another man tried to grab my legs, but I kicked out and heard him curse as my booted foot slammed into the man's jaw.

"Hold that fucker," the man growled, grabbing me around the neck while more hands held me down.

My vision started to dim but then the man in

charge forcibly removed the hands. "I don't want the fucker dead." He stepped back straightening his jacket. "Get him in the truck. *Now.*"

No way!

In a last ditched effort to get away, I yelled, *"Dad! Help me!"*

My dad paused.

They all did.

Then my dad took one step toward me...hesitated. A bullet hissed from beside me—a silencer muffled the sound—and I watched as my dad disappeared around the corner seconds before I saw brick from the building fly off.

He did it!

He left me!

"I'm not going with you," I raged against everything. The fact of what my dad had done, the restraints holding my wrists, the hands gripping me. I struck out, blindly, as I struggled and kicked. My teeth sank into the soft flesh of the hand covering my mouth and I felt a moment of triumph as the man cursed in pain. Seconds later, the triumph was gone as the man's fist flew into my face. I felt the pain blossom, starting on my nose as my mouth filled with the metallic taste of blood. The pain ricocheted through me as I turned my head to the side and spat out blood. It felt like my jaw was on fire while I breathed through the pain.

I sucked in a breath to fight harder but my body tensed as fingers dug into my cheeks as a hand clamped around my face. The man in charge leaned forward, his eyes burning with anger as he loomed over me. "You're mine now lad. You're going to become my fighting machine. No more fucking nursemaids. I'm going to make you a man, and you're going to make me money to pay off your father's debt."

I couldn't talk with the hand clamped around me, but I memorized the man's face, and made sure that I would never forget it.

That close to me I noticed the scar to the right side of his face that ran a good few inches. I thought that he was an American at first, but now I wasn't sure. Something else was in him, and his accent, one I couldn't place, slipped with his anger.

I hoped that when I woke up in the morning the memory of tonight would still be there. Because one day, when I was a man—stronger—I was going to get even with everyone involved…including my dad, the one person I always thought would be there to love and support me—the one person who was supposed to protect me from evil.

How wrong was I?

Evie (10 years ago)

WHILE MY MOM AND dad were partying with friends, and supporters of my father, I was on the sidelines trying to pretend my life didn't suck. I'd tried to fake a headache so I'd be allowed to stay home but it hadn't worked. I'd been told to sit and sip water regardless as to how late it had gotten.

I was twelve years old and hated that my father had just been elected as a state senator. My mother told me that I was selfish for thinking about myself all the time; that I should be more supportive.

How could I be more supportive when the new job meant my father would be away from home even more than he already had been? I really didn't see me wanting my dad at home as being selfish. I loved him, and missed him when he wasn't home.

But now, he would be gone more and school would be even harder to deal with. The other kids loved to make fun of me because of my family and my father's ambition.

I wanted to be part of a normal family. I couldn't even remember the last time we all ate around the table at the same time. I would only have my dad for family vacations now. He'd promised more but I knew that wouldn't happen. He loved his work, and really I should stop being ungrateful because I had everything I would ever want...apart from the one thing I *really* wanted...my father home.

My one best friend, Millie, was the only one who truly knew my fears, and she was the only person to know how much I hated my life.

Over the past few months I'd spent so much time at Millie's house that it felt like my second home. I loved being there. Her father was larger than life and, although he'd scared me at first, I'd finally gotten used to him.

My mother still tried to keep me apart from Millie when she wasn't lost in a world of her own making, and actually paid more attention as to what I was up to.

Like now.

I sighed as I spotted her walking toward me with a sour expression on her face, as though she'd eaten a lemon. It soon changed to a smile when Mrs. Grant appeared to her right.

Mom certainly had something on her mind though because her path continued toward me. I hated being center of attention, which she knew so I hoped that I wasn't expected on stage or anything while my father made his speech, even though I knew I wouldn't get away without.

"Evie dear." Mom took the cup of water from my hand and tugged me up. "Straighten your dress. Your father is about to make his speech and we both need to be at his side to show our support." And then she had to go and ruin it all. "We'll be on the front page of the newspaper tomorrow."

My heart sank and I wanted to run. I would have except her grip around my wrist tightened…almost to the point of being painful.

"Just be pleasant for the rest of the night, and," her lips twisted with annoyance, "I'll let you go on the trip with Millie and her family."

While her words sunk into my shocked brain, I let her lead me across the room to where my father stood with his team.

Mom knew how to get her way but I didn't for one minute believe she'd just thought about that to get me to do their bidding. She'd have something else up her sleeve and need me out of the way so that she didn't have a child to supervise. I wasn't about to complain because I wanted to go to Chicago with Millie more than anything. When I'd brought it up to Mom, she'd scoffed at the idea because she considered Millie's family beneath her. I couldn't see why she couldn't treat everyone the same.

"Smile," she hissed between her teeth.

And like the world's most lifelike puppet, I did exactly what she wanted. My smile was full of love and support as we greeted Father.

"There she is." His smile was real as he enclosed me in his warm embrace and I felt a pang of guilt that mine wasn't. "My princess," he whispered against my ear before he kissed the top of my head.

Available to purchase.

ABOUT THE AUTHOR

While Lexi is the author of the chick lit series, Tallulah James Mystery, and the fantasy/romance series, The Fifth Realm, she is also the author of over seventy novels. Based in Ireland, this British author has been writing since 2013.

Follow on social media:

Website: http://lexibuchanan.net
Email: authorlexibuchanan@gmail.com

facebook.com/lexibuchananauthor
x.com/AuthorLexi
instagram.com/authorlexib
bookbub.com/author/lexi-buchanan
amazon.com/Lexi-Buchanan/e/B009SPA94U

9 781918 152180